THE DEADLY TRAVELLERS

Kate began to speak rapidly. "I know you'll think I'm crazy, as everyone else does, but you do know something about Francesca, don't you? Please tell me. I can't get rid of the feeling that Mrs. Dix's death had something to do with her."

"Stuff and nonsense!" But there was a faint shine of perspiration on Miss Squires' brow. And it was very cold in the room.

"Where is she? Why is she hidden?"

"I know nothing," Miss Squires said loudly. The cat, alarmed, struggled in her arms. "I'm sorry, Kate. I'm upset. I still can't believe Mrs. Dix is dead."

"I think you do know," Kate said slowly. "You just won't tell."

Kate left the cottage as much frustrated as she was frightened. She knew the missing child, the dead woman, the attempts on her own life, were all tied together. But nobody would believe her. *And nobody would help her . . .*

Also by the same author

The Marriage Chest
Never Call it Loving
Siege in the Sun
Bella
Night of the Letter
Winterwood
Sleep in the Woods
Whistle for the Crows
The Bird in the Chimney
Samantha
The Vines of Yarrabee
Afternoon for Lizards
The Shadow Wife
Waiting for Willa
The Voice of the Dolls
Melbury Square
The Sleeping Bride
Cat's Prey

and available in Coronet Books

The Deadly Travellers

Dorothy Eden

CORONET BOOKS
Hodder Paperbacks Ltd., London

First published by Macdonald & Co. 1959
Coronet edition 1969
Second impression 1972

The characters and situations in this book are entirely imaginary and bear no relation to any real person or actual happening

Printed and bound in Great Britain for
Coronet Books,
Hodder Paperbacks Ltd,
St. Paul's House, Warwick Lane,
London, EC4P 4AH
by Hazell Watson & Viney Ltd,
Aylesbury, Bucks

ISBN 0 340 10787 1

ONE

THE HOUSE WAS on the outskirts of Rome, in a rather mean street which turned off the via Appia. There was a group of dusty cypresses on the corner, and then the row of shabby houses with their peeling paint and faded colours. Some children were playing in the dust. A woman flung open a shutter and leaned out to call something shrilly to them, and they scattered like disturbed sparrows.

In the other direction, towards the via Appia, the Street of the Dead, with its crumbling tombs and catacombs, there was a stream of traffic, fast cars, buses laden with sightseers, and noisy, impatient motor-scooters. It was no longer a way of peace for the sleepers in the tombs on the roadside, but then it never had been. Long ago it had rung to the marching feet of legions, or the shouts of the persecutors, and the weak cries of the crucified. In comparison, the screech of klaxons and the ear-splitting roar of the motor-scooters seemed harmless and innocent.

Perhaps the taxicab that was drawn up outside the house in this shabby street was also going about perfectly innocent business. The man watching in the shade of the cypresses would not have paid any especial attention to it if it had not seemed an unusual thing for a taxi to come to this kind of street. And to that particular house. So instead of strolling past casually he had drawn back to the slight cover of the cypresses and, with his hat pulled well down over his eyes, watched.

It was only a few minutes before the door of the house opened and a young woman came out. Tall, slim and attractive, she was the most unexpected sight of all, so far. For what would a fashionable young woman whose camel-hair coat might have been bought in one of the better Paris or London stores, and whose dark hair had a casual, expensive cut, be doing in this locality?

She was talking to someone out of sight. Presently a rather stout little girl dressed in a white frock, with a large blue bow in her hair, appeared and climbed into the waiting taxi. Behind her darted a thin, dark woman with a suitcase. The suitcase was placed in the taxi, the girl held out her hand to shake hands with the thin, dark woman, who, dressed in a faded cotton dress and scuffed-looking slippers, was the only person in this small scene who appeared to be in character, the only one who could have been expected to emerge from the shabby house in the rather furtive little street.

Then the tall girl climbed into the taxi, too, and the door banged. The watcher made an involuntary step forward, but he was too far off to hear the instructions given to the driver. He swore under his breath, then strolled studiously and casually in the other direction as the taxi whirled around and proceeded towards the city. As it passed him he caught only a glimpse of its two occupants, the fluttering butterfly bow in the child's hair, and the girl's dark head turned towards her young companion. But he heard the child's voice, shrill with excitement, "*Arrivederci*, Gianetta !"

So there was no more time to investigate the shabby house. Now perhaps there was no need to. Fingering the worn covers of the notebook in his pocket, remembering the scribbled address of this house in this street, and the cryptic added note "*might be using a child*," he hurried to the busy highway and impatiently waited for a taxi.

It was impossible to be certain where the previous taxi had gone, but by the child's luggage, and the girl's air of haste, one assumption could be made.

When at last he was able to secure a car, he gave the driver his destination, "*La stazione, pronto!*"

The driver nodded his head, grinning with wicked pleasure at being given a free hand to mow down as much of the traffic as possible. At his destination the man cursed again, this time at Mussolini and his grandiose schemes for building such a superb railway station that made one cross acres of floor-space before reaching the train.

As he had expected, it was the Milan train just due to depart. Indeed, it was at that moment pulling out. He had to elbow people out of his way, and run for his life to get on the last carriage.

"Bravo! Bravo!" called a porter, white teeth gleaming, dark eyes ashine.

But the man was not amused. Did the Italians consider all contests with speed and danger, so long as they themselves remained onlookers, a pleasant diversion? Did that explain a great deal of their mentality?

Perhaps it did. Perhaps that was why he was here.

A good-looking young woman, probably English, and a child. . . . And that other face that it was not possible to forget, for a drowned face, even had it been that of a stranger, was not an easily forgettable sight. And this had not been a stranger's face. . . .

TWO

THAT MORNING TWO days ago in London, Kate did not see Miss Squires, as usual. The girl at the desk of the little employment office with its provocative title "Job-a-Day," and in smaller letters "Also Objets d'Art procured," said in a slightly awed voice that Mrs. Dix herself had asked for Kate when she came in. Would Kate wait while she found out whether she could go up now?

It had been William who had first suggested Kate going to Mrs. Dix. William, who was as practical as Kate was impractical, said that if Kate planned going on living in London (as she certainly did) she would have to supplement her very precarious employment as a commercial artist. So why not do the odd jobs, such as taking out old ladies, or poodles, meeting trains at melancholy stations like Liverpool Street, doing

Christmas shopping for the bedridden, or even baby-sitting, providing the brat wasn't too spoilt and loathsome.

This suggestion of William's had turned out excellently. It provided Kate with three or four days' employment a week, which, added to the earnings she made from her drawings, enabled her to keep the basement flat in West Kensington. She was attached to this flat chiefly because of her landlady, Mrs. Peebles, who was as endearing as a poised tomahawk and just as stimulating. With Mrs. Peebles lurking about the house, life was as full of surprises as Kate liked it to be. In addition to the satisfaction of earning extra money, she found the work with Mrs. Dix interesting and enjoyably unpredictable. Also, she had got several excellent sketches of strange old-lady faces, Rembrandt style, and had some rather enchanting drawings of dogs skipping about Kensington Gardens, among the blowing autumn leaves and the chrysanthemums. These she hoped to sell.

Apart from the money angle, she found it made life pleasantly interesting, not knowing, each time she visited Miss Squires, solid and placid in her little dark office under the stairs which led up to the so far unseen apartments of Mrs. Dix, what strange task awaited her, whether it were catching a train to Southampton to meet an elderly American couple, or to go to the Portobello Road market to search for a specified piece of junk required by a client.

Mrs. Dix, until this morning, had remained a mystery. Miss Squires hinted at a Tragedy. Fifteen years ago Mrs. Dix's husband had been missing on a secret mission, some hush-hush task that could only be mentioned in the sacred precincts of M.I.5, and the poor lady still refused to believe that he was dead. She got up every morning with the renewed optimistic conviction that this would be the day he returned home. She kept his bed aired, a plentiful supply of food and drink, and contrived, Miss Squires said pityingly, to infuse into her cluttered rooms an air of excited expectancy. It was very sad, because after fifteen years there was really no hope. There had been that body washed up on the coast of Portugal that had never been positively identified, but there was little doubt that it had been that of Major Dix. If it hadn't, then there was the Iron Curtain, and no one was likely to survive fifteen years of that. Anyway, there had been not a word, not even a rumour of an unidentified Englishman in some Siberian prison. Not even a question in the House. So it seemed that Mrs. Dix, poor soul, would go on living in her fool's paradise.

But until this day, Mrs. Dix, who had infused her special brand of eagerness and eccentricity that was almost genius into her business, had remained as invisible as her husband. At least, to Kate, one of her minor employees. No doubt she gave audience to the important people, the ones entrusted with special jobs such as shopping for the Prime Minister's wife, or the ones who requested, not a warming-pan to be turned into some kind of barbecue business, or an umbrella stand that would adequately hold flower arrangements, but the Faberge chess set last heard of in Alexandria, or the late duchess' diamond and ruby tiara which one had heard was being sold....

Admittedly, these last were rare requests. Miss Squires, who liked Kate, sometimes became a little less reserved and imparted a breathless rush of information, about acquiring skeletons for medical students, and other macabre objects. It was tragic that although Mrs. Dix could acquire white camels from Arabia, or pearls from the Great Barrier Reef, she could not find her missing husband. But she still refused to admit that he lay in an unnamed grave somewhere along the banks of the River Tagus.

Reflecting on all this, Kate was a little nervous about at last meeting the fabulous lady. Passing Miss Squires' room on her way to the narrow stairway, she heard Miss Squires call, "Is that you, Kate? Special mission for you today. It'll be a nice jaunt."

Kate stuck her head around the door of the dark little office, "Where am I to go?"

"None of my business, dear. But you'll enjoy it. Lucky girl."

The room in which Mrs. Dix sat was a quite ordinary

living-room, a little over-furnished and with an extravagant number of bowls of flowers. It did not in any way resemble an office. Mrs. Dix sat on a faded, green velvet couch.

She was a very plump lady with prematurely white or bleached hair, in, perhaps, her early fifties, though her extreme plumpness and her white hair may have added an unnecessary ten years to her age.

She wore brown velvet, with a little ruching of lace at the throat. She was, Kate thought, like a chocolate meringue.

Her smile was winning. She waved a dimpled hand towards a chair. "Sit down, my dear. Forgive my not getting up. My heart, you know. The doctor forbids any exertion. You're Kate Tempest, aren't you?"

"Yes, Mrs. Dix." Kate obediently sat down and refused the proffered box of chocolates.

"Oh, not just a little one, dear?" Mrs. Dix cried, disappointed. "Try this knobbly one. It'll have a nut. Not so bad for the figure. Though really, I do assure you, you have *no* need to worry. You're a sylph, positively. Now me, I'm past redemption. But I do so adore chocolates."

She beamed at Kate. Her cheeks were delicately pink, her eyes a faded blue, benign, a little far-off, as if her visitor were not quite real to her, but that instead she was looking beyond, to the door, which might open at any moment to the one she wanted to see above all.

"Now, you're wondering why I've sent for you, of course. Miss Squires has told me about you. She says you're reliable, sensible, sophisticated, not likely to lose your head in a crisis."

"Thank you," Kate murmured bewilderedly. William had always said exasperatedly that reliability was her least obvious quality, but neither Mrs. Dix nor Miss Squires knew her as William did, and it was her business to see that they never completely achieved this knowledge.

"Most important, those qualities," Mrs. Dix emphasized. "Now tell me a little more about yourself. You live alone?"

"Yes." Though one could hardly call it living alone, with Mrs. Peebles' watchful eye and attentive ear, overhead.

"Family?"

"Only a stepmother who lives in the country."

"How do you get on with her?"

"She's perfectly sweet, but I only acquired her when I was eighteen, so naturally she's not deeply interested in me. Since my father died she has taken up growing flowers for the market. Even when I visit her she forgets I'm there. She's cutting roses, or transplanting polyanthus, or something."

"Marriage plans?" Mrs. Dix asked in her friendly, inoffensive voice.

Kate thought of William and said definitely, "Not at present. None at all."

"Well, that all seems very satisfactory. It leaves you completely free to do these things for me. I like to know my employees are without urgent family ties, when I send them on jobs abroad. Shall I tell you what I have in mind for you? It's a very important mission, but actually very simple, and only requires travel sense and, of course, responsibility. You've been on holidays abroad, Miss Squires tell me."

"Yes, several times." On a shoe string, of course, staying at pensions or youth hostels, walking blisters on to one's heels, living on rolls and spaghetti.

"Splendid. Have you been to Rome?"

"Once only, for two days."

"You don't speak Italian?"

"Almost none at all."

"Well, that won't matter greatly."

"But what am I to do, Mrs. Dix?"

"Oh, a very simple little mission indeed. You won't have a chocolate? I shall, I'm afraid. My husband is to blame, you know. He indulged this passion of mine. I shall tell him, when he comes home, how he is to pay for it, with all these pounds of flesh." Mrs. Dix chuckled, squeezing at her plump waist. "My dear, you have beautiful blue eyes. With that black hair. Quite arresting."

Kate sighed. "Yes, but my nose is wrong." William's healthy outspokenness never allowed her to become conceited.

"Not seriously wrong. I'm wondering if Miss Squires is right, after all. Are you the right person to send? But if you're used to travelling, and you promise to behave with discretion—" Mrs. Dix's pale blue eyes suddenly flew up, looking directly at Kate instead of at the distant door. "Rather a pity, isn't it? Well, never mind. It's a very simple thing we want you to do. Merely to bring a child, a little girl, to London. You are to be her courier, in fact, or her nannie, if you prefer to look at it that way." Mrs. Dix's plump fingers dipped into the box of chocolates again. She leaned back on the couch smiling benignly. "Well, my dear, how do you like the idea of that?"

Kate privately liked it very well indeed. Her one brief trip to Rome had filled her with a passion for that ancient and fabulous city, and the chance to go back, with all travelling expenses paid, seemed too good to be true. Instinctively, she began to look for the flaw in the plan.

"May I ask you some questions, Mrs. Dix?"

"Indeed. Go ahead."

"Who is this child? An Italian?"

"Yes; of divorced parents, unfortunately."

"Does she speak English?"

"A little. Very little, I believe."

"How old is she?"

"She's seven, only a baby, poor pet, and her name is Francesca. I can visualize her, can't you, dark-haired, shy, unhappy."

"Why unhappy?"

"Because her parents are fighting over her. That's the story, you see. The court granted the mother, who now lives in London, custody, but the father wasn't having any of that, so what does he do but nip over to London and kidnap the child. Quite illegally, of course. So there has been more action about that, and now he has agreed to give her up. But someone has to come and get her and travel back to England with her. Naturally, a child of seven can't travel alone."

"Why doesn't the mother go?"

"She's just recovering from an illness, brought on by all this worry. She won't completely recover until she has her child again. So see what a good deed you will be doing, besides seeing your beloved Eternal City again."

Kate hadn't said that it was her beloved Eternal City, but refrained from pointing this out. Indeed, she was beginning to feel pleasantly excited and stimulated. Perhaps she could arrange with Mrs. Dix to go a day earlier than planned, and have one free day in Rome, to wander about sketching the wild flowers growing tenaciously in the centuries-weathered walls of the Colosseum, the gargoyles, with their noses rubbed flat, on old cathedrals, and the hurrying people along the pavements, silhouetted against the ancient splendour.

"Well?" said Mrs. Dix, with her comfortable smile.

"I'd love to go," Kate said enthusiastically. "But—"

"You're wondering about your fee? I think you will be quite happy about that. Francesca's mother is prepared to be generous. Considering the exertion and responsibility, we thought twenty guineas, and expenses paid. You'll travel first-class both ways, and there'll be a night in Rome when, of course, you must be comfortable. Comfort's such a necessity, isn't it?" Mrs. Dix's fingers hovered over the chocolate box.

"But, Mrs. Dix—"

"Aren't you happy about the fee, my dear?"

"Yes, indeed. I think it's very generous. It makes me feel Francesca must be a very important child." Or a very difficult one, she thought to herself.

"A bone between two dogs, a poor little creature. Then I take it you agree to go?"

"I'd absolutely love to. But can I see Francesca's mother first?"

"Rosita? Whatever for?"

"I'd like to talk to her. If the child can't speak English we may have trouble about the sort of food she likes, and so on." She refrained from adding that she wanted dearly to see Francesca's background, to get a complete picture of the situation. Was her mother really ill—or just lazy?

Mrs. Dix hesitated. She said doubtfully, "I shall have to see. I shall have to ring Rosita. But yes, of course, I think it is a very good idea. She would like to see you, too. After all, it is her child whom all this fuss is about. Yes, I think that can be arranged. I'll let you know."

But was it Kate's imagination that now, all at once, Mrs. Dix's pale blue eyes did not quite meet hers?

Kate didn't know why she had this curiosity to see Rosita. Was it because the child, Francesca, the unknown little Italian, a bone between two dogs, as Mrs. Dix had called her, wouldn't seem real until she had talked to her mother? Or was it because she imagined Rosita to be a spoilt, olive-skinned beauty with hypochondriac tendencies, and wanted to see for herself who most needed sympathy, the bereft mother, or the father, obviously emotional and affectionate, who had come to England to swoop up his daughter and fly with her.

It was probably foolish of her to risk getting emotionally involved in the problem of two strangers, but all her life she had never found it possible to stand aside as a spectator of other people's happiness or unhappiness. She had always plunged in, to share or sympathize. It had not always been rewarding, and William constantly warned her that her quixotic tendencies would finally lead her into some inextricable and insoluble problem. Kate didn't worry much about that. It made life exciting and unpredictable, and one owed it to people to be interested in them.

As she went down the stairs from Mrs. Dix's room, Miss Squires poked her head out from her small dark office.

She was a little rotund person with shortsighted brown eyes and an anxious forehead. She had taken a fancy to Kate, and twice had invited her to her prim little cottage on the Sussex downs, where she lived alone, except for a large black and white cat called, unimaginatively, Tom.

"Are you going to do it?" she whispered, as if, all at once, she was nervous of the plump, chocolate meringue woman in the room upstairs.

"Oh, yes. It's wonderful. Perfectly wonderful."

The corrugations in Miss Squires' forehead deepened. "I

thought you'd think that. Actually, it was I who suggested giving you the job. You're reliable, and I thought the poor kid would like someone young and gay."

"How nice you are!" Kate said sincerely.

Miss Squires, middle-aged and plain, and obviously unused to compliments, flushed.

"I said nothing but the truth. But I hope it will be all right. This trip," she added.

"Why shouldn't it be? Oh, you mean Francesca might be unmanageable?"

"That, and her father. We don't know about him, you see."

"But if he's promised to let the child go."

"Yes, of course."

"And I'm going to see the mother this afternoon."

"Oh, well, then—"

As Miss Squires hesitated, Kate laughed. "I do believe you're one of those old-fashioned people who don't trust foreigners!"

Miss Squires flushed again and said gruffly, "Not always without reason. Well, take care of yourself. Come down to the cottage for a weekend when you get back."

Rosita lay on a couch in a high-ceilinged, luxurious room in a house in Egerton Gardens. She was small and dark-haired, with a pointed, sallow face, and eyes that made Kate think fleetingly of Raphael's "Portrait of a Woman." It was not so much that they were full of secrets, as that they would like to seem so. No doubt this pose was quite successful with men.

She did not look particularly ill, Kate thought. Her languid hand-shake seemed to be a pose, too.

It was true that she was merely spoilt, probably disliking the thought of the long journey to Rome, or not wanting to risk another encounter with her ex-husband.

There seemed little doubt that he would not be the only man in her life.

Kate looked around the room, noting the couch with its pale green brocade covering, the curtains of rich crimson Italian damask, the gilt-framed mirrors, the cushions and small tables. Was this a good environment for a child of seven —a tense, unhappy and probably maladjusted child? With a hypochondriacal mother lying on a couch extending a languid hand to callers?

She spoke in English that had only the slightest accent.

"Miss Tempest, it is so good of you to come to see me. Mrs. Dix told me how thorough you are. That you want to find out about Francesca before the journey."

"It's a long journey," Kate said.

"You are so right. That's why I can't possibly go myself, much as I would like to. But I really can't stand it. All this upset has made me ill. Antonio behaving like this—"

Her face puckered as if she were going to cry. She hastily controlled herself. If she were not ill, she was extremely nervous, Kate thought, and wondered why. Although the reason seemed obvious enough. A kidnapped daughter, and all the entailed fuss.

"You'll find Francesca a very good child, Miss Tempest. Even a little—how do you say it—solemn? She won't give you any trouble. She doesn't speak much English, but enough to get by. She's well-grown for her age. Oh, and don't forget her doll. She must always have her doll or there are fireworks at bedtime. Miss Tempest, you will take good care of her, won't you?"

"Of course I will."

"Mrs. Dix said you could be trusted. I wish I could go myself. I might have flown, but Francesca's crazy, but crazy, about trains and boats, the Channel ferry—ugh!—and the Eiffel Tower."

"The Eiffel Tower?"

"Yes, she adores going up it. To the very top. I hope you have a head for heights. I haven't."

Rosita shuddered, and Kate suddenly wanted to laugh. This was going to be a light-hearted odyssey after all, with a child who adored continental trains, and Paris from the top of the Eiffel Tower. Now she had become a person, and a person of definite character. Suddenly Kate was looking forward to meeting her.

"Why are you smiling?" Rosita asked suspiciously.

"I like the Eiffel Tower, too."

"Good heavens! How very extraordinary! Then the two of you should get on very well."

"Indeed we will," Kate said cheerfully.

She got up to go. The limp hand came out again. But this time, to her surprise, it clung to hers with surprising strength. It was cold and a little damp. It was, strangely enough, like the hand of a person who was afraid....

Mrs. Peebles had to be told, of course. Apart from her grudging but fairly accurate delivery of telephone messages, she liked to know what Kate was up to. Since all Kate's visitors had to come through the front door and negotiate the stairs to the basement they had to endure the sharp surveillance of Mrs. Peebles, and this was another source of interest for that lady who was frank and uninhibited in her comments.

"That young man last night, Miss Tempest. Bit of a weed, wasn't he? You can do better than that," or, "She'd be a flighty piece, that Miss Edwards. Pity the man who gets her."

Of William, surpisingly enough, she approved, which was rather boring. Kate felt that a few waspish comments from Mrs. Peebles would have made her fly hotly to William's defence, and perhaps have made her fall in love with him. As it was, they disagreed about almost everything, from the latest play to the colour of William's tie. William was slow in his movements, and untidy and forgetful, and appallingly frank about either Kate's work, her appearance, or her behaviour. He treated her, she complained bitterly, as if they had been married for years. But somehow they stuck together. Or rubbed along. And the odd, weedy or more flamboyant types of whom Mrs. Peebles disapproved did not take her out a second time. Perhaps it was this quality of outspokenness that drew Mrs. Peebles and William together. Whatever it was, Kate suddenly felt enormously relieved at the thought of escaping, for a brief time, from both of them.

Mrs. Peebles was sharp, small and spry. At the sound of the front door closing she appeared, like a mouse from the wainscoting, ready to dart back into her hole the moment she had seen all that was necessary.

"Oh, it's you, Miss Tempest. Only one message. From Mr Howard. He said to tell you to keep tomorrow night free because he had tickets for the Old Vic."

"He'll have to take someone else," Kate said pleasantly. "I'll be halfway to Rome."

"Rome! Whatever do you want to go there for?"

"Just a job. I'll be away about three days, so if anyone rings—"

"Oh, yes, scribbling away at that telephone when I should be doing my work. Then you'd better ring Mr. Howard."

"Later," said Kate, going towards the stairs.

"He'll be around."

"Not if I know it. I have to pack and have an early night."

"Rome!" muttered Mrs. Peebles. "What are they sending you there for? Turning you into a spy?"

"Something like that," Kate said cheerfully. "Just my cup of tea, don't you agree?"

The early night was not possible, for, as predicted by Mrs. Peebles, William did come around. He was a tall young man and heavily built. Kate's one armchair sagged perilously beneath his weight, and although she had a reasonable amount of floor space, his comfortably sprawled legs formed a constant hurdle as she tried to do her packing and cope with his barrage of questions.

"It's fishy," he said.

"Don't be absurd. What's fishy about bringing a seven-year-old child to England?"

"Why don't they let you fly?"

"I've told you. Because Francesca loves trains and wants to go up the Eiffel Tower. It's a special treat."

"She sounds like a spoilt brat."

"She probably is, but for twenty guineas pin-money I'd travel third-class to Greece and back. And they're giving me time in Rome to rest. I'll be dashing madly about, of course. I want to get a good face for my new illustration."

"For the hero? An Italian?" William said sceptically.

William edited a small, highly literary, topical magazine himself, and was often irritatingly facetious about Kate's endeavours in the romantic field.

"No, for the villain. Someone madly wicked and irresistible. I'll probably fall in love with him."

"Don't do that," said William mildly, tapping out his pipe and scattering ash indiscriminately.

"Why not?"

"You wouldn't be happy."

"I suppose you think I'm more likely to be happy with someone like you, cluttering up my flat, criticizing me, wearing foul ties, needing a haircut—my God, you do need a haircut!"

"I'll go out and get some beer," said William.

"You won't come back here with it. Honestly, I haven't time. Please go so that I can concentrate on what I'm doing."

"All right. I can see when I'm not wanted. Want me to come to Victoria in the morning?"

"For heaven's sake, no!"

"Then I'll meet you when you come back. Send me a postcard or something."

"I'll have the child then, and goodness knows what."

"If the 'what' is an Italian count, I can always punch him in the jaw."

"Don't be absurd! Only three days and travelling all the time. And with my face—"

"Even with your face. Snub nose, crooked mouth. You're an ugly, adorable little devil."

He didn't take her in his arms in a civilized way, he swooped over her like a great tree whose branches suddenly engulfed her. Tweedy, redolent of stale pipe smoke, strong....

Kate struggled impatiently and ineffectually, then submitted. Really, it was too boring. Why did William have to be so masterly?

THREE

FRANCESCA. THE NAME conjured up the picture of some dark, thin, flashing-eyed temperamental child, full of charm and animation.

Kate was frankly taken aback when she met the real Francesca. Just as she had been taken aback at the sight of the street and the house where she had been instructed to pick up the child.

Her mind flashed back to Francesca's mother, lying languidly on a couch in a luxurious room, and to the excellent arrangements made for her own trip to Rome, the good hotel at which she had spent the night, and the ample money she had been allowed.

Francesca, obviously, was a valued and much-desired child, and her parents not lacking in means. Why, therefore, was she living in such a squalid house? Even temporarily.

And why was she in the charge of such a dirty, down-at-the-heel woman as the one who came to the door in response to Kate's knock?

It was late autumn, but still hot in Rome. Kate had undone her travelling coat, and her hair was ruffled from her nervous gesture of pushing it back when she was agitated. She thought the taxi-driver had brought her to the wrong street. She looked at the row of shabby, paint-peeling houses in astonishment, and hesitated to get out and knock on the door of Number 16.

When the woman, whose quick smile seemed to hide uneasiness, opened the door, she was even more sure she had made a mistake. Yesterday, exhausted by her long journey, and yet determined to make the most of this brief visit to one of her favourite cities, she had rushed from the Colosseum to Hadrian's Arch, and then to the Borghese Gardens, and late in the evening had done a tour of the fountains. Tiredness and excitement had given her a queer feeling of being transported to the past, to the days of hungry lions turned on living human flesh, the crack of the slave-driver's whip, and the cries of a rabble demanding a victim. This morning, when her journey to get Francesca had taken her so near to the Appian Way, the mood had persisted, and she was temporarily haunted by a heavy sense of decay beneath the splendour, and of death.

But the woman in the shabby little house, strangely enough, was expecting her. Apparently she had come to the right place.

She called in a shrill high voice, "Frances-s-ca !" and took Kate inside, although she said in halting English that the child was ready, and had been for the last hour.

The dark little room in which Kate stood smelt strongly of garlic. She wondered hazily, with yesterday's tiredness still hanging over her, whether this woman was now married to Francesca's father—but surely the elegant and expensive Rosita had never come from surroundings like this.

The woman was explaining something in a gabble of Italian when the little girl came slowly in.

Kate had another surprise, for this stout, heavy child with the heavy-lidded sullen eyes, was utterly unlike the Francesca she had imagined. It seemed, however, that within the fat little chest of the sulky and silent child there must dwell the phantom of Kate's imagined Francesca, for she had chosen to wear, of all things, a white organdie dress, elaborately starched and ironed, and in her straight dark hair was a huge stiff bow.

She was a little girl going to a party where, despite all her parents' attempts to make her decorative and appealing, she would remain clumsy, silent and hurt.

She was pathetic.

Kate realized it at once, and went quickly towards her.

"Francesca ! Hullo !" Her voice was warm and gay. "My name is Kate, and I'm taking you to your mother. But first, of course, we have the train journey, and a visit to the Eiffel Tower, and lots of good things to eat."

The child surveyed her stolidly and mutely. The woman shook her head. "She does not understand. She speaks very little English. And you, signorina?"

"No Italian," said Kate, laughing. "Never mind, we'll get along. Is she ready? Does she have to say goodbye to anyone?"

"No, no. That is all done. Her papa yesterday when he brought her here. I was her nurse, you understand? He did not wish the last farewells."

She made the motion of wiping her eyes, and Kate had a moment of sympathy for the absent emotional father who perhaps was the more deserving parent. For it was a little difficult to imagine this child fitting into the London drawing-room of her attractive mother.

She felt uneasy and a little sad, and had to remind herself that none of this was her business before she could take the child's soft broad hand and say, "Then we're all ready, Francesca. Your bags?"

"Just this small one," said the woman, handing Kate a rather battered and cheap-looking suitcase. Then she swooped over the child to give her a hug. The child stiffened, and backed away. The woman hugged her, nevertheless, then had to straighten the preposterous blue bow and the unsuitable dress.

She shrugged her shoulders. "She would wear that dress, signorina. I know it is foolish, but when Francesca insists...." She shrugged her shoulders again.

Looking at the stubborn, unmoved face, Kate could very well understand what she meant. There might, she feared, be more than one silent battle before the two of them reached London. This probably explained the generous fee she was to receive. Well, never mind, she would earn it....

"The taxi's waiting," she said. "We'd better go. Thank you, signora...."

The child walked quite placidly beside her. She hadn't spoken a word.

They were stepping out into the brilliant sunlight when suddenly the woman gave a shrill cry and called to them to wait. She darted away, saying something that sounded like "bambino," but when she appeared a moment later she had only a quite small doll in her hands. It was not a particularly attractive one. Its blonde hair had become stringy, and its silk dress was slightly grubby. It didn't even look as if it had been an expensive doll, the kind one would have imagined parents like Francesca's would have lavished on her. But apparently it was her much cherished one, for Kate remembered now that Rosita had said she would never go to bed without her doll.

Nevertheless, such was her stolidity, that when the woman thrust it into her arms, she held it almost indifferently, and indeed for two pins would have dropped it on the doorstep. However, she was still holding it as she climbed into the taxi, and it was there, too, that she found her tongue, and called in almost as penetrating a voice as the woman's, "*Arrivederci*, Gianetta."

In the train the two of them faced each other warily across the narrow space of their first-class compartment.

"Is this your first trip to England, Francesca?"

Since her sudden boisterous goodbye, Francesca had remained stubbornly silent in the taxi, behaving, when Kate spoke to her, as if she were stone deaf.

But now she suddenly broke her silence and said flatly, "No spik *Inglese*."

Oh, dear! thought Kate. Was that true? Or were those heavy-lidded eyes that made the child look like a junior Mona Lisa hiding secrets? Surely, with Gianetta, her nurse, speaking English fairly fluently, and her mother speaking it very well indeed, she would have learnt at least a few words. Kate decided this was more than probable, and before the journey was over she would have caught her out. In the meantime, she would chat pleasantly, whenever necessary, and pretend that it was of no importance whether or not she were answered.

"We'll be having lunch shortly. Do you like eating on a train? I still think it's one of the most exciting things to do. Next to sleeping on one, of course. When you wake up tomorrow morning you'll be practically in Paris, practically at the foot of the Eiffel Tower."

Francesca's eyes suddenly flew wide open and a gleam of excitement showed momentarily in them. This was no proof that she had understood anything except the last two words, but it did show that she set great store on her visit to the Eiffel Tower. She began to spread her dress carefully about her so that it would remain fresh and uncrushed for so important an occasion. No doubt it was for that purpose that she had insisted to the disapproving Gianetta that she would wear her party dress.

Going up the Eiffel Tower represented a party to her. Probably it was the only real thing that emerged out of the confusion of her separated parents and her loss of security. Encouraged by this success, Kate persevered with the conversation.

"What's your doll's name?"

The Mona Lisa look came back. Kate picked up the doll lying rather forlornly on the seat, and pointed to it.

"Who?"

"Pepita," said Francesca sulkily, then suddenly snatched the doll from Kate and clasped it possessively.

"That's a Spanish name."

"Si."

It didn't seem to matter. The doll, with its ragged blonde locks, was obviously the only other object of Francesca's affections. The Eiffel Tower and a shabby doll, and a white organdie party dress and a festive blue bow in her hair. All at once, strangely, Kate wanted to cry.

The train rocketed on through the dry autumn countryside towards Milan. Kate tried out her few Italian words on the waiters in the restaurant car. Her charge remained silent except when at one stage she made a long excited speech to one of the waiters.

The man grinned. Kate asked, "What was all that?"

"She says she like ravioli, signorina."

"And there's no ravioli?"

"Only spaghetti, signorina."

The waiter shook his head regretfully, and Francesca stolidly but expertly wound enormous quantities of spaghetti into her mouth. She was a philosophical child. She made the best of what she could get. No doubt her short life had already taught her that necessary lesson.

No one came to share their compartment. Towns, in an afternoon haze of tawny roofs and old, sun-faded walls, went by. There was more arid countryside and shabby villages, with splashes of paint, orange and violent blue. Francesca had dozed after lunch, her doll clasped firmly on her spaghetti-filled stomach. Now she was wide awake.

"We change trains here to cross the frontier," Kate explained at Milan. "Then we change again at Basle, and there you'll have a bed for the rest of the night."

She didn't know whether the child understood, but she came docilely to climb off the train and follow Kate through the jostling, excited, noisy mob that was Milan railway station. She was a plump incongruous little figure in her now crushed white organdie and nodding blue bow. At least, Kate thought, those foolish clothes made her too conspicuous to get lost.

But with her lumbering docility, that was like that of an elderly and faithful dog, it did not seem probable that such an emergency would arise.

The man with his hat still pulled too low over his eyes changed trains at Milan, also. While Kate fussed about finding their compartment and getting Francesca safely on board he, however, had time to make a telephone call.

Although, since it was a trunk call, it seemed at the last minute that it wouldn't come through in time, and he was tensing and untensing his long, nervous fingers in impatience and anxiety when at last the clerk called to him.

"Your Swiss call, signor."

Then it took some time to make himself understood. After all, it wasn't an ordinary call inviting himself to stay overnight because he happened to be passing through Basle. It was something very different.

But at last he thought all was well.

He paid for the call and walked away slowly, reflecting on the split-second timing required, the crazy improbability of the whole thing.

Then a thought came into his head and his eyes narrowed and grew grim. This had to succeed.

Once more he had to run for the train. It very nearly left without him. Cursing the way Continental trains deliberately sneaked out of stations as if trying to leave passengers stranded, he sprinted after it and just hauled himself on board.

Kate left Francesca for a few minutes to go and wash and try to revive herself. Her enthusiasm and expended energy had caught up on her, and now she was very tired. She hoped Francesca would sleep when she finally got her bedded down in the Paris train, because she herself was going to sleep like a log.

Her face, pale with fatigue, looked back at her from the blurred mirror. Only a trickle of water came from the tap into the not-particularly-inviting basin. She would have to make do with a little coolness on her temples and a freshening of her lipstick. After all, did it matter, with only Francesca's hooded eyes to look at her?

Certainly she would have dinner in the restaurant car at Basle. But even then, all alone, with Francesca safely tucked in bed, travel stains could not matter less.

Francesca was sitting bolt upright when she returned to the compartment.

"Man," she said succinctly.

"A man?" Kate looked at the other unoccupied seats. They had been lucky so far, having a compartment to themselves. Not many people seemed to be travelling first-class on this train.

"That's all right," she said. "Other people can sit in here if they wish to."

The child's eyes looked burningly at her, and she spoke in her rapid, incomprehensible Italian.

"Did he talk to you?" Kate said. The child did not seem frightened, only wide awake and interested. Someone apparently had had a conversation with her in her own language, and it had cheered her up. Perhaps this stranger would come back and talk in English, too. In the meantime the barrier of their different languages was between them again. Francesca, rocking her doll in her arms, had found someone she had liked. Perhaps, taking after her mother, she responded more to men than to women. At least it had made her find her tongue for she said something else, ending with "Londre."

"London?" said Kate sharply. "Did he ask if you were going to London?"

"Londre," said Francesca again, and held up two fingers.

"Two," said Kate, puzzled. "Twice?"

But did she mean the stranger had been to London twice, or that Francesca herself had?

Surely this rather comic-opera journey with the doll, the organdie dress and the Eiffel Tower looming ahead, as a lure, had not happened previously!

At Basle there was slight pandemonium, for a party of schoolgirls from the ages of seven to twelve boarded the train, and there seemed to be confusion about their seats. There was a great deal of arguing and chattering going on, and the two mistresses in charge of them, after talking emphatically to an ever-growing group of railway officials, at last shrugged their shoulders fatalistically and herded the children on board.

Kate, with her passports, baggage and her small travelling companion safely passed by the Customs, found their two-berth sleeping compartment and went into it thankfully. Francesca by this time was more than three parts asleep. Kate produced the bread and the cheese she had bought at Milan, anticipating the child's inability to stay awake for late dinner in the restaurant car, but even these Francesca was too tired to cope with. She gnawed at the bread for a while, then yawned widely and clambered into her bunk.

"Oh, not in your dress!" exclaimed Kate. "If you sleep in that it will be quite ruined."

But her endeavours to make the sleep-drunk child sit up

and be divested of the now sadly crushed organdie were useless. She did not intend to have her dress removed. Either she was genuinely asleep or she was foxing, and Kate was even less able to cope with her stubbornness than the absent Gianetta had been.

Actually, she didn't think Francesca was foxing, for her doll, Pepita, lay forgotten beside her, and she had the gnawed piece of bread still clutched in her hand. She was just worn out, poor little thing. After all, although she hadn't responded to any friendliness, neither had she complained. There had been no tears or whimpering, which represented rather astonishing self-control for a seven-year-old. One had to remember that.

But that dress was going to be a travesty by morning. Kate opened the shabby little suitcase to see what Gianetta would have considered Francesca's requirements on the journey. To her relief she found a blouse and skirt and a light tweed coat. Somehow the blouse and skirt would have to be forced on to the child in the morning, or, as a last resort, the coat could cover the crumpled dress.

So all would be well. The worst part of the journey was over. By morning they would be in Paris and by evening in London. Kate pulled the blanket high around Francesca's sleeping face, and switched off the light over her bunk. Now she would relax with some food and a glass of wine in the restaurant car, and then get some much-needed sleep herself.

It was quite a journey to reach the restaurant car, and she was thankful the train had not yet left the station. For she had to step over little clumps of schoolgirls who, apparently just as weary as Francesca, had bedded down in the corridors, anxiously supervised by the two harassed mistresses.

One of the mistresses, a young girl with a round, freckled, hot face, said indignantly to Kate, "There's been a mistake over our reservations, so we have no seats at all. Can you imagine? And we've been travelling all day. The children are worn out."

"They look it," said Kate sympathetically. "Can't you find any empty seats?"

"Oh, we've parked a few of them here and there. There are thirty of them, and only two of us to look after them." She pushed the damp hair off her forehead and sighed. "Oh, well, as long as no one falls over them. Kids sleep anywhere. But I do think these Continental trains are the end!"

Kate thought of the turmoil in the morning when everyone wanted to get into the toilet at once. She picked her way down the narrow corridors, over the children, over stacked luggage, past standing passengers, and the bitterly harassed official with the list of couchettes, past crowded compartments packed with weary tourists already trying to find welcoming spots for their heads, even if it were their neighbour's reluctant shoulder. Twenty guineas, she was beginning to think, was not such a generous fee after all. Someone struggling on to the train dug the corner of a suitcase into her shin, and behind her the sorely tried official said in tones of the greatest entreaty to an importuning woman, "*S'il vous plâit, madame . . .*"

Then a man, leaning against the window, suddenly smiled at Kate.

His eyes were dark and intense. "Some scrimmage," he said.

She assented wearily. Then suddenly she laughed back at him. It was funny, after all, and they were both English being amused at the ways of foreigners.

The fragmentary encounter cheered her up. Also a savoury smell indicated the nearness of the restaurant car. She came into its comparative emptiness and quiet, and, shown to a seat by a courteous waiter, she sat down and relaxed with pleasure.

She had only glimpsed the man's face. But she was quick at faces. Almost now she could have sketched it. It had been dark and narrow and, for he did not seem old, surprisingly deeply lined. In repose, she guessed, it would be aloof and withdrawn, but his smile brought it to life.

If the sitter for Titian's "Head of a Man" in the Louvre had suddenly smiled, he would have looked like that, she thought.

She fumbled in her bag for her pencil, and began sketching on the menu the waiter had given her.

Soup was brought, and when she looked up the young man was sitting opposite her.

He smiled. "Do you mind?"

"Not at all."

The train was moving now. Suddenly she was aware of the strain the day had been, and the deep relief she felt now that the journey was so far accomplished. The lights swayed a little to the rocking of the train, and it seemed to her that the face of the man sitting opposite her swayed a little, too, blurring and becoming clear again. She was very tired indeed.

"You're travelling to England?"

"Yes. By ferry tomorrow."

"So am I. We may see one another again."

Was he going to be the "romantic interest" of her trip? But it was a little too late in the journey to have this happen, and there was all day tomorrow to be occupied with shepherding the silent Francesca about Paris. Besides, it was a pity she was so tired.

"You've been on holiday?" went on his pleasant, polite voice.

"No, on a job. Well, a sort of job. It gave me an excuse to get to Rome again."

"Tell me your favourite part of Rome."

"The Colosseum, I think. On a sunny, windy day, when the wild flowers are blooming in the cracks of the walls."

"And you don't hear the lions roaring any more."

She nodded. "Just silence and peace."

"Everything's the same in a thousand years. It doesn't really matter much if you missed your chariot in A.D. 80 or your train in this year of grace."

His eyes were dark and sparkling, but his mouth had a definite line, and there was a certain grimness to the deeply-scored lines in his cheeks. He could be anything, anybody, a philosopher or a buccaneer.

"That's a rather dangerous philosophy," Kate said.

"Is it? Would you care to share a bottle of wine with me?"

"Thank you. I'll probably go to sleep, but I suppose that will be the same in a thousand years, too."

"Even Helen fell asleep." His eyes on her were frankly admiring. More wide awake, she might have felt a little embarrassed. Now it was mildly pleasant to toss the conversational ball to such an entertaining stranger.

"My name's Lucian Cray," he said.

"I'm Kate Tempest. Not so romantic."

"Romantic?"

"Yours is a little, isn't it. Actually it sounds like a stage name. You don't mind my saying so?"

"Not in the least. After all, Shakespeare could have known you and called you Miranda."

She laughed. "Don't be absurd. Not with my nose!"

The waiter had come with the wine list. They both discovered they preferred vin rouge, and somehow this seemed another bond between them. Another one? Kate puckered her brows. What was the other bond? That somehow she knew intuitively Rome affected him in the same way as it did her. The settled dust of long ago pandemonium, and the peace of old stones....

She realized that he had taken the menu from her and was studying her sketch.

"Do I look such a haggard individual?"

"That wasn't intended for you to see."

"Clever. If this is a habit of yours, you could become a menace."

"I know. But faces fascinate me. If I don't put them on paper they seem to stay graven on my mind."

"So that's what you've been doing in Rome, looking for faces of gladiators."

"And the ones Michelangelo and Leonardo da Vinci used to discover. They're still there, you know. If you sit in the via Vittorio Veneto, they all pass by, the beggars and the misers, the corrupt and the crafty. If you changed their clothes you'd find the Pharisees in the Temple and the Caesars and the Judas's, the hungry and the lonely and the good."

He poured wine into her glass.

"I've travelled for nearly three days," she said. "I'm beginning to talk nonsense."

"On the contrary. I wish you'd go on."

"No, my job is drawing, not talking. Have you been on holiday?"

"I had to see some people in Rome," he said, with what seemed to her deliberate vagueness. "Ah, well, Paris tomorrow, then London. Perhaps I'll see you in London?"

"Aren't we getting on a little fast?"

He smiled, with that sudden, disconcerting look of rakishness. His eyes were brilliant and bent only on her, but there was a certain coldness, almost a calculated look to them.

"Yesterday the Roman gladiators were only just around the corner, today the twenty-first century looms over us. Too fast? My dear Kate!"

She began to laugh. The wine and her tiredness and the movement of the train made her feel as if she were on a merry-go-round, a very gay, fast one whirling her towards some inevitable destiny. He began to laugh too, touching her hand, and suddenly she was light-heartedly, unquestioningly happy.

She did not think of William at all.

She left him at last. She had to get some sleep in order to cope with Francesca the next day. But she knew she would see him again, perhaps at breakfast, perhaps on the Channel boat, perhaps in London. . . . He still hadn't told her anything more about himself except that slightly unlikely name. But that didn't matter. She would find out. There was plenty of time.

People and luggage still cluttered the corridors of the train. Kate made her way back to her compartment, carefully picking her way among the piled bags, the weary passengers, and, in her own carriage, two knots of sleeping schoolchildren.

The jolting of the train bumped her against a man standing near the door to her compartment. He turned to say "Pardon!" He was smoking a large cigar. He looked at her with bold, dark eyes. She frowned a little, knowing she would have to pass him again, with her sponge bag, on her way to wash—if one could pick one's way over sleeping bodies to the toilet. There would be the squeezing past again, the murmured apology.

But she was wrong. When she came out again he had gone. She had to stand in the rocking corridor in a dispirited little queue for fifteen minutes, and was thankful all the time that Francesca was fast asleep. She had not stirred when Kate had entered the compartment. There was the unmoving plump hump of her beneath the bedclothes in the shadow. She'd probably wake frightfully early, and, sleep-dazed and out of temper, Kate would have to cope with her objections to wearing anything but the crumpled white organdie.

Well, no use in anticipating trouble. Live in the moment—in this particular moment of watching the miserly trickle of water coming from the faucets, and seeing in the swaying speckled mirror not her own face but that of her dinner companion, dark-eyed, sombre Lucian Cray. It was not a name one would forget. Or a face....

In spite of her extreme tiredness, she did not sleep well. She dozed, and woke with a start every time the train jolted to a stop. Somewhere behind these drawn blinds and this stuffy little room a world existed. One heard it in the shouted names of the stations, ringing through the abruptly still night, like battle honours. Then the more mundane chattering of late travellers, the slamming of doors, the sliding forward and the increasing rhythm of the wheels again, lulling her to uneasy sleep until the next jolt came, and the voices from another world shouted. Once there was scuffling outside her door, and one of the schoolgirls whimpering. The soothing voice of the mistress calmed her. Thank goodness her own charge was much too stolid and placid for upsets. She slept like a log. Once Kate leaned over from her bunk to see the tuft of hair unmoving on the pillow. If only she could sleep as soundly herself.

But the night passed in this uneasy, half-conscious dozing, and when the first light crept through the edges of the drawn blinds her head was still tight with exhaustion and her eyes felt full of grit. She sat up to reach for her hair brush, and at that moment the pandemonium started outside her door.

It was those wretched schoolchildren again. There were their concerted voices, all speaking at once, and above them that of one of the mistresses who was obviously begging for quiet.

"Now, if you'll all just stop talking for a moment and listen to me. Mary, you say Annabelle was beside you when you went to sleep."

"I thought she was, Miss Rickerby, but Helen says she saw her go to look out of the windows at the other end of the corridor."

"But she came back, Miss Rickerby, because I saw her fixing her coat to put her head on."

The mistress was obviously getting a little panicky.

"Didn't I tell you all to stay here and not move."

"But sometimes we had to go—"

"Oh, I understand that. Annabelle isn't there now, is she?"

"No, we told you. There's a man in there shaving. He's taking simply ages."

"Never mind him. We must find Annabelle. Miss Jones has Laura and Jennifer and Caroline, and there are four in the compartment at the end of the corridor where some kind people let them sleep on the floor. How many of you here?"

"Eleven."

"So Annabelle is missing. Then she must be in one of the compartments. I'm afraid we'll have to knock politely at doors and ask people."

At this stage, Kate climbed out of her bunk, and pulling on her sweater and skirt, opened the door.

"Are you in trouble? Can I help?"

The young mistress, whose round, freckled face was hot and flushed again—had it remained so all night, or was it permanently so?—looked up quickly.

"One of my charges seems to be missing, but she can't be far away. It's all right, really."

"You poor thing," said Kate sympathetically. "I have only

one to look after, and that's responsibility enough. You with all these."

"It would have been all right if our reservations hadn't been muddled. Still, we're through the night, aren't we, children? When we find Annabelle and we've all had some breakfast we'll be as right as rain."

"What does Annabelle look like?"

"She has red hair—"

"And freckles," echoed the children.

Kate smiled. "She should be conspicuous enough. I'm sorry I haven't got her under my bunk. Shall I help you look?"

"Oh, no, thank you. We can manage very well. She wouldn't possibly have left this carriage. Actually she's rather a timid child. I thought she was dead asleep when I saw her last. She must be in one of the compartments. I'll just take a quick look. I'll give you a shout when I've found her, if you like."

"Yes, do."

Temporarily giving up ideas of a wash, Kate went back into her compartment and shut the door. Francesca would wake any minute, but one might as well let her sleep as long as possible. It was only six o'clock. She would leave the blinds drawn and rest a little longer herself. The poor girl with all those children to look after. No wonder one of them had gone astray.

But she couldn't be far away. Children didn't disappear off trains unless someone deliberately pushed them off.

And now it was tomorrow, and there was Francesca, and the Eiffel Tower, and later the ferry to Folkestone, and perhaps a glimpse of Lucian Cray somewhere in the crowd, perhaps that flashing smile of his across a multitude of heads.

Kate dreamed pleasantly as the light grew, and through the chink of the blind she could see the stubble and the faded tawny look of the gentle French fields. Grey clusters of houses, leaf-stripped trees, white horses browsing on the autumn grass, and occasional fairy-tale turrets, or the glimpse of a white château among groves of beeches.

But a little later her reverie was broken by an apologetic tap on her door.

"Who is it?"

The young mistress, even hotter of face, slid the door back and put her head in.

"I'm so sorry, but there absolutely isn't a sign of Annabelle. Do you mind awfully if I look in here? I'm sure she wouldn't hide herself away uninvited, but just in case—"

"Of course. Look where you like. But there's only Francesca here. She's still asleep. You can see."

"Oh, I'm so sorry—honestly I'm at my wit's end—"

"It's time Francesca woke up anyway," said Kate, and pulled the blinds up with a clatter. "There, now you can see for yourself that I've no redhead—"

But her words died on her lips. For the sound and the light had woken the child in the bunk, and she turned sleepily, lifting her tawny head, opening pale green eyes, and showing clearly her face with its comic mask of sandy freckles!

The child was not Francesca at all. She was the missing Annabelle, who, recognizing her hot-and-bothered schoolteacher, began to smile, revealing two missing front teeth. Smiling an idiot's grin, Kate thought frantically, as she began to realize the dreadful implication.

It was not the tow-haired Annabelle who was missing. It was Francesca!

FOUR

THE GIRL *was* an idiot, Kate thought furiously. For she seemed to have no idea how she had come to sleep the night comfortably in a first-class compartment while her schoolmates huddled miserably in the corridor. She said she had gone to sleep beside Mary and just woken up here. That was all.

"What was your little girl like?" the schoolmistress asked sympathetically.

The past tense, thought Kate, with renewed anger. As if Francesca were dead!

"She's dressed in a white organdie dress, and she has a large blue bow in her hair. She's Italian and speaks almost no English."

She was aware of the young mistress, smug now that she had the full count of her pupils, eyeing her with the faintest scepticism. Perhaps it did sound an unlikely description of a child on a long journey, but that wasn't her fault. Anyway, she had Francesca's modest suitcase, with the more conventional clothes in it, to prove that everyone wasn't quite mad.

She dived under the bunk to produce it. But it wasn't there. At least, not where she had put it. It must be in the rack—or somewhere. In her exhaustion last night she had moved it, and forgotten.

"What are you looking for?" asked the other girl.

"Francesca's suitcase. I thought I put it under the bunk. It must be here somewhere."

In a panic she was dragging the blankets off the bed, lifting the mattress.

But there was nowhere in a small railway compartment that a suitcase could be completely concealed. The fact was too obvious to deny. Both Francesca and her belongings were gone. They had simply vanished into thin air.

"How very odd!" murmured the young mistress, the scepticism in her eyes. In the narrow doorway she was now surrounded by curious, peeping children. Frantically, Kate searched their faces, round ones, long ones, heavy ones, grubby ones. But there was no small Mona Lisa, no hooded, secretive eyes that told nothing.

"She *must* be on the train somewhere," Kate said.

"Well, she shouldn't be hard to find in those clothes. But she's not in this carriage, because I'd have noticed her when I looked for Annabelle. Would you like me to help you?"

"Oh, if you would!"

"Of course I will. The children will help."

"Her name's Francesca, and I'm taking her to London to her mother. She doesn't even belong to me, you see. That makes it more awful. I left her in the bunk fast asleep when I went to have dinner last night, and when I came back she hadn't moved. At least—" That must have been when the strange thing had happened, when the sandy-haired Annabelle had got into Francesca's bunk and Francesca had gone off—or been taken off. Because she could swear no one had come into the compartment during the rest of the night.

"It's a pity Annabelle doesn't remember anything," the other girl said. "But she always was a sleepyhead. I'll get Miss Jones to help, too. Surely with all of us we'll soon find her."

The children thought it was a game. They surged through the train like a small tornado, shouting, "Francesca!" and bursting unceremoniously into compartments, squalid in the growing light, with tossed bedding, luggage, and half-awake, unshaven, tousle-headed travellers.

Kate, following in their wake, asked politely but urgently if anyone had seen the little girl in the white organdie dress. Everywhere she was met with blank faces. No, no one had seen such a child. A white organdie dress! But that one would remember. What had happened? Had the child been kidnapped? But that would be impossible on a train. She must be somewhere.

Yes, Kate agreed feverishly. She must be somewhere. But where? And why had she disappeared?

An irate guard, trying to stop the avalanche of children, demanded to know what was happening, and Kate explained what the trouble was, first in English and then, seeing he was only half understanding, in her careful French.

"You say the child was in the bed when you woke this morning?"

"But not the same child, I'm trying to tell you."

His eyes popped slightly. He was short and rotund, and looked quite stupid.

"M'selle, children do not change overnight."

"You don't believe me! But it's true! Someone must have changed them over. One of the schoolchildren, a completely strange child, was in the bunk."

"Ah-ha! A joke, m'selle. You have a friend on this train who likes to play jokes?"

"I don't have any friends on this train," Kate snapped impatiently. "And it isn't a joke. Or if it is, it's a monstrous one."

"You have the little girl's bags, perhaps?"

"No, they're gone, too."

The little round, popping eyes surveyed her with what was now becoming familiar scepticism.

"M'selle, you are sure you began the journey with a child? You did not just imagine a little girl in a white dress with a blue ribbon in her hair?" A creature from a fairy tale, a figment of the imagination. . . . That was what he was saying to her.

"Or perhaps she flew out of the window!" he suggested with heavy jocularity.

There was a hand on Kate's shoulder.

"Kate! Is there some trouble?"

It was Lucian. Kate almost flung herself into his arms.

"Yes, there is. I've lost Francesca."

His forehead creased with concern. But even his concern, she could see at once, was not serious. Or was she getting into the state where she suspected everyone?

"You didn't tell me anything about a Francesca last night. Who is she? Your poodle?"

"No, she's not a poodle. She's a child. Seven years old, and dressed in white organdie, with a large blue bow in her hair." She went over the familiar description wearily, and waited for the inevitable reaction.

But she was grateful to see that he didn't think the description so improbable. He said quite seriously, "A child of seven wouldn't get off the train by herself, unless she fell off, and that's even more unlikely. Have you looked right through the train?"

"Almost."

"Then let me help you with the rest. Which way?"

"This. It's awfully good of you. I *must* find her before we get to Paris because there, in the crowds, it wouldn't be so difficult for someone to whisk her away."

He turned in the swaying corridor to look at her.

"Why should anyone do that?"

"She's the child of divorced parents, and they're fighting over her. I was bringing her to England."

"Ah! Spies!"

"Lucian, don't joke! It's serious."

"I'm not joking." He put his hand back to take hers. She found the pressure of his cool, strong fingers immensely reassuring. In that moment, in the muddle and worry and exhaustion, she fell very briefly in love with him.

Suddenly she was remembering the man whom she had bumped into in the corridor the previous night, standing near her compartment and turning to give her that long, insolent look.

Perhaps he was the person who had substituted Annabelle for Francesca, and then, with enormous confidence, lingered to see whether she would notice the change-over when she went to bed.

But *why* would he do it? And if he had done, he must have Francesca on the train somewhere. Unless he had left at one of the stops during the night, when the phantom voices had called, and everything had seemed to be happening in a dream.

The children came bursting back to say that there was absolutely no sign of any little girl in a white dress on the train. They had looked *everywhere*, even in the toilets, and the guard's van.

One of the mistresses followed, nodding her confirmation. "I'm awfully sorry. But it does all seem so strange, doesn't it?"

She meant that none of it was real. And neither did it seem real, in the cool, growing dawn, with fatigue-marked passengers making their way to the restaurant car for coffee and rolls, and others snapping suitcases shut, and preparing for their arrival in Paris.

Kate pressed her hands to her forehead. Was she awake or in a nightmare?

"Kate—you did have this child with you?"

The schoolmistress had looked sceptical, the little French guard, stout and stupid, had looked sceptical, the passengers with their dull, sleepy eyes had shaken their heads with a polite lack of belief. Now, as the last straw, Lucian, who might at least have been the one to help her, looked disbelieving also.

"Do you think I was drunk and imagining things? Of course I had her with me."

He was not smiling now. His face had its sombre, rather gaunt look.

"You didn't mention her at dinner last night. I thought you were travelling alone."

"I'd put her to bed. She was fast asleep. I didn't tell you everything last night. Should I have?" Her brows were raised haughtily. She was no longer in love with him. She hated him. He must know she was frantically worried, and yet he chose to think she was inventing a fantastic story about travelling with a child and losing it.

"You have her luggage, perhaps, her passport?" he said gently.

"No, I haven't. That's disappeared, too. Believe it or not!"

Curious passengers were listening now. She seemed to have eyes staring at her from all directions. She thought she would lose her difficult self-control and begin to scream.

"Find her for me!" she begged in a whisper. "Ask me questions afterwards."

No little girl in a white frock! No little girl in a white frock! The answer seemed to come automatically from all around.

Suddenly Kate saw the man whom she had bumped into the previous night. He was still looking at her with his sly, dark gaze, but when she burst out accusingly, "Have you seen a little girl in a white dress?" he shook his head and said in bewilderment, in a broad Bradford voice, "Ee, have you lost one?"

No one with a voice like that should look so sinister. It was so unexpected that it was wildly funny. Kate thought she must be going mad. Then the train seemed to spin dizzily, and she had to grip the window ledge.

Lucian's hand was on her elbow.

"Are you all right, Kate? You'd better come and have some coffee."

"I can't. Not without Francesca. She needs coffee, too."

"We'll be at the Gare du Nord in half an hour. Ten minutes for coffee isn't going to affect Francesca one way or the other, but it is going to stop you from fainting."

"Lucian, what am I to do?" she implored.

"Have coffee and we'll talk."

It was useless to talk, of course. She could only repeat how she had put Francesca safely to bed in the lower bunk the night before and then had had that moment of utter horror and disbelief on seeing the strange child's face in the morning.

"Freckles! Missing teeth! And she hasn't a word of explanation."

"She wouldn't have climbed in that bunk if it hadn't been empty."

"You mean she deliberately got in herself?"

"I should think so. Half asleep. Looking for somewhere to be comfortable. Naturally she isn't going to admit she remembers."

"But, Lucian—" She gave him a long look over her coffee cup. "You still don't believe me, do you? You think it's I who have been dreaming up things."

"Have you Francesca's railway ticket?"

"She wanted to keep it herself with her passport. She's an experienced traveller. Everything was in her suitcase." Kate pushed away her coffee cup and stood up. "What on earth am I going to tell her mother and Mrs. Dix?"

"We're coming into the outskirts of Paris," Lucian said. "Look."

Kate took an anguished look at the slate-grey roofs, the amber chestnut trees, the slowly awaking streets. Clasping her doll, determined and silent, Francesca was to have made her promised ascent of the Eiffel Tower....

How *could* she have disappeared into thin air? She couldn't. That was nonsense.

Kate stood up decisively.

"The moment we arrive, I'm getting the police."

It was impossible, in the fuss and bustle of arrival, to see whether anyone anywhere was trying to smuggle a fat complacent child off the train. Although she hung out of the window to get a good view of the moving people, the shouting porters, the babble of several languages made her feel only baffled and confused. The two schoolmistresses, with their clutch of children anxiously shepherded, passed by. One of them looked up.

"We're terribly sorry we can't stay to help. But we can't risk losing any of our own."

"That's all right," Kate called.

"So sorry about all that mess up. . . ." They were pushed out of sight. The man from Bradford, hurrying past with brief-case and raincoat, paused to give her a wink and his sidelong glance. But the business man in him was already uppermost, and he had forgotten her trouble. The train was almost empty now. It seemed useless to search the empty compartments littered only with orange skin and cigarette butts.

If Francesca were there she would be making her presence known—if she could still speak. . . .

Suddenly, in a flash of illumination, Kate was remembering the child's efforts last night to tell her that a strange man had talked to her. Someone interested in her, someone who had excited her, and told her something that pleased her. Her eyes had been shining.

Had he been making an irresistible bribe to her? Had he asked her to get off the train when he came for her?

Because now Kate was convinced the change-over of the children had been made while she was having dinner with Lucian.

Francesca must have been taken off the train at the last minute before it left Basle, but her abductor naturally would not want Kate to discover her absence until morning. So the sleep-drunk Annabelle, luckily to his hand, had been substituted....

"Kate," came Lucian's voice, "there's no use in waiting here."

Kate turned slowly. "What am I to do?" she asked again.

"Call the police if you like. But I doubt if you'll convince them a child existed. I suggest you should first put a call through to London and get your instructions from there."

"Yes. I'd better telephone Mrs. Dix. But however am I to tell her. . . ." She felt dazed now, with worry and exhaustion. She was temporarily content to have him lead her.

"Put your coat on. Where are your bags?"

"There's only one. Francesca's—" Her voice trembled. She made herself say carefully, "You're very good to me, although you don't really believe there is a Francesca. I've got some gloves somewhere—oh, look!" Her cry was chiefly one of surprise, as if she, too, had been becoming convinced that Francesca did not exist. "Here's Francesca's doll. It's got pushed behind the mattress. There you are! That proves she was here!"

Triumphantly she held up the slightly shabby doll, pathetic and somehow without personality now that it lacked an owner.

"You have to believe me now," she said.

"Any child can have a doll," he murmured. "But, Kate dear, I've never disbelieved you. Come along, let's get off this ghastly train."

Francesca lured somewhere on a false bribe, without her promised trip to the Eiffel Tower, without her precious doll. A little girl determinedly dressed for a party that seemed to be fast becoming a tragedy. . . . Kate resolutely swallowed the lump in her throat and followed Lucian.

They had to wait for the London call to come through. Lucian had arranged it. He had somehow got several talkative and gesticulating railway officials persuaded of the urgency of it, and had also the tired and irritable guard, who had first heard Kate's report of the child's disappearance, to bear witness. They all stood and watched as Kate at last got through and heard Mrs. Dix's voice which seemed to come from infinitely far away. Yet even in that wispy sound she could hear the breathless eagerness of the "Yes! Yes! Who is it, please?" and she realized the forlorn and fantastic hope that was running through Mrs. Dix's mind. Even after fifteen years of silence, any telephone call from abroad revived her tenacious optimism. This, perhaps this, was the one to tell her that her husband had come back from the dead....

It was cruel to shatter that expectancy, and even in this emergency Kate hesitated.

"It's Kate here, Mrs. Dix."

"Kate? Kate?" The disembodied voice had lost its liveliness. It sounded groping and lost, as if the transition from hope to reality was too much for its owner.

"Kate Tempest, Mrs. Dix. I went to Rome to get Francesca."

"Oh, yes, I remember. The Italian child. What about it? Where are you speaking from? Has something gone wrong?"

"Terribly wrong, I'm afraid. Francesca's missing. Lost. She disappeared off thc train. And no one has seen her."

They were all watching her in the dreary brown room, Lucian, the telephone operator, and the officials who had argued and protested that the whole thing was imaginary, unnecessary. Relatives had picked up the child at Basle—if there had been a child.... Pouf, anyone could leave a shabby toy on a train....

"Missing! Oh, goodness me!" The flurried voice told Kate that Mrs. Dix was groping in a convenient chocolate box for sustenance.

The disappointment that the call from abroad was not from her long-lost husband after all, and now this news that Kate's mission had gone so badly astray, would throw her off balance.

"Shall I call the police in? That's what I must know."

"Those foreign police—so excitable—just to find a child who's run away. Can't you look for her?"

"You don't understand, Mrs. Dix. She's been missing all

night. We think she was taken from the train at Basle."

"We?"

"The gentlemen here," Kate said, looking placatingly at the avidly listening gentlemen. "The railway officials, and an Englishman who has been very kind."

There were sundry strange noises coming through the receiver that may have been Mrs. Dix clucking in alarm, or merely munching a chocolate. But when she spoke again her voice was surprisingly decisive.

"Not the police yet, dear. Must get in touch with Rome, with her father. Oh, dear! What a bore! And we thought you so reliable. Miss Squires said—dear! dear! Not those dreadful foreign police, making an international incident out of it. Wait there till I call you back. What's your number?"

"Can I get a call here?" Kate whispered frantically.

This was the signal for a great deal more arguing to go on, but finally it was agreed that if it came in a reasonable time it would be permitted. It was the best that could be done. Sitting in the stuffy office waiting for the telephone to ring, catching the hostile glances of French officials who thought her infinitely careless, to say the least, to lose a child on a journey—if there had been a child—Kate realized what the note beneath Mrs. Dix's breathlessness and alarm had been. Not disappointment. Fear.

Or had she imagined that, too? Had she imagined everything, even the small shabby doll, Pepita, packed now in her capacious handbag?

But the second call, when it came, was complete anticlimax. Mrs. Dix's voice bubbled over with reassurance.

"Kate dear, not to worry. Everything's all right. Francesca's home."

"In Rome?" Kate gasped.

"Yes, with her father. He's very bad and quite unscrupulous. When she had gone he suddenly decided he couldn't bear it, or perhaps it was spite against Rosita, of course, but he telephoned some friends in Basle and had Francesca taken off the train. At a moment when you were not observing, of course."

"But how extraordinary!" Kate gasped.

"Isn't it?" Mrs. Dix's voice was full of cheerfulness. "He's nothing better than a brigand. Giving you all this worry, poor Kate. Rosita is broken-hearted, naturally. She wants you to stay in Paris for a day just in case we have any further instructions for you. Go to the Hôtel Imperial in the Rue St. Honoré. And get a rest. You must be worn out. We'll call you there if we need you. And fly home in the morning. Miss Squires will arrange for your air ticket to be sent to the hotel."

"Mrs. Dix, are you sure Francesca's all right?"

"I can only tell you what that rogue has told me. And *quite* unashamedly. He thinks he's very clever, in fact. But in case he should repent, which is unlikely, Rosita thinks you should stay until tomorrow."

"I've messed it up so badly."

"My dear, no one could have anticipated this. You said there was an Englishman?" Mrs. Dix's voice lilted naughtily. "And you're in Paris. Go and have fun."

Kate put the telephone down slowly. She gathered that everyone listening had got the gist of the conversation, for there were wreathed smiles and shrugging shoulders.

"What did I tell you?" said the now affable guard. "She flew out of the window, pouf!"

"It has been a storm in a soup plate, no?"

It was only Lucian who was not smiling. He was looking at her with a long, curious, thoughtful look, neither surprised nor relieved at the solution to the small drama, but rather as if when he had persuaded her to ring London he had known exactly what the result would be. And almost as if it amused him a little.

But why should it be amusing? She herself felt remarkably far from mirth. For apart from the pathos of it—Francesca, lonely and bewildered, snatched away from her promised party, deprived of her favourite doll, and bundled back to Rome, like so much merchandise, probably to the rather grim Gianetta and the squalid little house off the via Appia—there had been that strange note of fear in Mrs. Dix's voice.

Even during her second call, when she had bubbled over with cheerfulness, Kate had calmly and uneasily sensed the apprehension. What, in the foolish and abortive episode, would make her afraid?

FIVE

THE GENTLE CLICK of the door opening aroused Kate late in the afternoon.

"Who is it?" she asked sleepily, not fully aware of where she was, or why she had been asleep when afternoon sunshine was still filtering through the windows.

There was no answer.

She sat up, blinking and looking at the closed door. But she was sure it had opened. That was what had woken her. Had someone come to the wrong room?

Or had someone been walking about softly in here, and left hastily when she stirred?

Fully awake, Kate sprang out of bed and hurried to the door. The corridor was empty. Somewhere she could hear voices speaking in rapid French, and on the ground floor she heard the lift gates shut. These were normal enough sounds in an hotel and nothing to get perturbed about.

Funny. She had been sure something had aroused her. Perhaps it had been the door of the next room opening and closing. Anyway, here was the day almost gone, and she had not yet had more than the glimpse of Paris that she had got on the brief taxi journey from the Gare du Nord to the hotel. Lucian had brought her here. He had told her to get some rest, and, if his business permitted, he would telephone her before eight o'clock that evening. He had been very kind. He had seen her through that nightmare hour when she had been searching uselessly for Francesca. But there was no reason why he should go on being responsible for her. She had realized that in the slightly withdrawn quality of his voice when he said goodbye to her. As if an unexpected duty had been safely discharged.

Well, he had thought the whole thing a hoax, anyway. He still did not seem entirely to believe that there had ever been a child, in spite of her conversation with Mrs. Dix, and in spite of the doll, which could have belonged to one of the schoolchildren.

Kate shrugged as philosophically as possible. After all, it could be Lucian who had been the ghost. He was even more transitory than Francesca. The only record she had of him was the sketch she had done on the menu card, and that was not particularly good. She took it out of her handbag to look at it again. His remarks about it were right, she thought, as she looked at the incomplete lines. He did look haggard and grim, like someone engaged in a losing battle or a lost cause. She would tear this up and forget it. And him.

But this she could not quite bring herself to do. She left it lying on the dressing-table, and picked up the telephone to ask for a bath. Her exhaustion still clung to her, and it made her feel strangely sad and gloomy. She had made such a mess of her mission to Rome, and the thought of Francesca, an innocent seven-year-old, caught up in quarrels that were not hers, depressed her. The child should be having the normal fun and security one associated with childhood.

However, a bath and fresh clothes, and then a quick excursion around Paris would take away her morbid feelings. The hotel was old-fashioned, and she was escorted, with ceremony, by an elderly porter with a towel draped over his arm, to the top floor where the bath was filled almost to overflowing with very hot water.

In this she lingered longer than she had meant to. When she returned to her room she wondered if Lucian had been trying to get her on the telephone. But it was foolish to stay in on the chance of a call from a virtual stranger who by now was probably too busy with his own affairs to worry about her. She would go out for a brief sight-seeing tour while the daylight lasted.

But it was a pity. . . . His face remained persistently in her mind. That sketch—where was it? She thought she had left it on her dressing-table. She was positive she had. But it was not there.

Neither did it seem to be anywhere else, not even in the wastepaper basket. Someone must have come in to tidy up the room.

But nothing else had been touched. The bed was left rumpled from her long sleep. Her things were flung carelessly about. With a small stirring of uneasiness she remembered the real or fancied opening of her door as she awoke from sleep. Had someone wanted to come in then, but finding her there, gone away? It would be difficult to know whether or not anyone had searched her suitcase, for its contents were already untidy enough. Her handbag she had prudently taken up to the bathroom with her, so her money and passport were safe. Only the menu card, quite valueless, was missing....

In the Luxembourg Gardens a little girl was trying to catch a kitten, but it had escaped and somehow climbed the statue of the Cyclops hanging over the Fountain of the Medicis. The dark, still water, sprinkled with amber leaves and flashing with the amber shine of darting goldfish, separated the child from the kitten. Her face had a lost, longing look. She instantly made Kate think of Francesca, and the look that would be on her face now that she had lost her doll and her party. Surely something could be done, even by an outsider, to make that child happy. She must talk with Mrs. Dix when she returned to London.

Meantime . . . the lovely slender queens with their flowing stone draperies stood in their calm circle round the plots of red geraniums, the grouped nannies and babies, the autumn-leaved chestnuts and the fountains. Some of the little girls playing on the grass wore starched white frocks. Kate found herself walking closer to them to look into their faces. How foolish she was not to be able to get it out of her mind that somewhere, somehow, Francesca really was in Paris. Perhaps having her promised ascent of the Eiffel Tower. . . .

Of course. That's where she should go before the light faded. She took a taxi, and was whisked across the city at an alarming speed. In spite of it being late afternoon there was still a crowd of tourists lingering about the preposterous erection, and the lifts creaking up and down were packed.

But as soon as she had arrived Kate realized what a forlorn and useless thing she was doing. Francesca was not here. Even if she were mysteriously in Paris whoever had seized her would not be the kind of person who would indulge her desire to ascend the Eiffel Tower.

A lift had just opened to disgorge its occupants. An official was saying beguilingly to Kate, "Ticket, m'selle. The view is marvellous. Such a clear afternoon."

Still in her dreamy and slightly haunted daze Kate went to the ticket office and bought a ticket. After all, the man was right. One might as well see the view. She filed into the lift with the waiting queue of people, and the doors shut. Slowly the creaking mechanism worked, and the city began to fall away. Kate edged to the side to look down. Suddenly she saw a flash of white in the crowd below.

"Kate! Kate!"

The lift creaked louder and around her people chattered excitedly in various languages. Kate wanted to shout frantically, "Be quiet! Be quiet! Someone's calling me!" She was gripping the side of the lift which dragged her inexorably away from the glimpse she had caught of a white frock.

Oh, if only they would stop it! *Had* someone called her? Now, as the crowds on the ground grew smaller it was impossible to know. Certainly a child had called. But had the name been Kate? Or was that her own wishful thinking? And thousands of little girls in Paris wore white dresses.

"Crazy structure," said a friendly American voice beside her.

Kate smiled vaguely at him, and began to push her way towards the doors.

"You had enough already?" his voice followed her.

The lift shuddered to a stop at the first floor. Kate pushed her way out. "Excuse me. I have to hurry. Excuse me." They would think she was ill, or had no head for heights. It didn't matter. Now she could run down the steps and be on the ground in a few minutes.

But would that be soon enough to know whether, indeed, a little girl had called excitedly to her?

She hurried out into the leisurely gaping and chattering crowd. She called "Francesca!" in a voice as high and shrill as any Italian's. But apart from people looking curiously at her, and another American, a woman, saying sympathetically, "Have you lost someone, dear?" nothing happened. The cry to her had been an illusion.

Or if it had not, Francesca had been taken swiftly away....

Now, all at once, Paris was beautiful and hostile, and for the first time she had to fight against tears. She felt as if she were in the middle of some strange, fascinating, lovely but treacherous nightmare. The Seine, dark and smooth beneath its high banks and bending trees, the gladioli glowing in the street-sellers' stall, the wandering tourists, priests, soldiers, and thin girls with long hair and secret faces were all part of it. She must get back to her hotel with its shabby, warm, red carpets and glowing brass, where Lucian might be waiting for her, and she could disperse the nightmare.

It was not Lucian who was waiting for her. A completely strange man stood up as she came into the foyer. He eyed her tentatively until the clerk at the counter nodded to him. Then he went over to her.

"Miss Tempest?"

"Yes." Kate was surprised. Why should this stranger approach her? He was certainly English. Apart from his voice, everything about him from his tweed jacket to his clipped moustache, rather plump ruddy face, and air of confidence, proclaimed the fact.

"I'm Johnnie Lambert," he said. "I got into Paris this afternoon, and Mrs. Dix suggested I look you up. She said something about a spot of bother."

"I don't follow—"

"Of course you don't." He took her arm in a friendly way. His voice was slightly hearty. But he looked pleasant enough, and he was not part of the nightmare. That was the important thing. "Come and have a drink and I'll explain."

He took her into the bar, and asked her what she would drink, then before she could answer said, "We're in Paris, so let's have something typically French, eh? How about a Chambery?"

He was undoubtedly the masterful type. But kind. And she needed someone like that just now to despatch the nightmare.

"I'm beginning to follow," she said, as he sat down with the drinks. "You work for Mrs. Dix, too."

"That's right. I've just had a spell of tutoring two young Arab princes. Glubb Pasha stuff in an academic way. But I'll be glad to get back to London, I'm telling you!"

"In the Arabian desert?" Kate asked, thinking that of course this was exactly his sort of thing. Schoolmastering with a difference, the tweedy-sporty type, full of good humour, fond of a dash of adventure, not quite middle-aged, and never allowing himself to admit the approach of that time.

"No, Beirut. Fair enough, but it palls. I just got in this afternoon, and when I rang Mrs. Dix to report she told me about you. We're flying home on the same plane in the morning, so she thought I might cheer you up. Said you were worried. Something went wrong with your trip. What was it? A disappearing child or something?"

"Sounds like a magician's trick," Kate said ruefully. "I don't see how I could have prevented it, even if I'd held her hand all the time. If her father insisted on her going back to Rome, who was I to refuse to let her go?"

"Quite. Quite. Matrimonial squabbles are the devil. But it was hardly fair on you, playing a trick like that. Is the father an Italian opera singer or something? Sounds like a love of melodrama. Did the child just disappear without leaving any trace?"

"She left her doll, which is another thing that worries me. She was very attached to it. I've been carrying it around in my bag."

"Her doll, eh? Well, that's proof, isn't it. Too bad. Poor little devil. Well, not to worry, Mrs. Dix says."

"Yes, I try not to, but I keep thinking of it from the child's point of view. So bewildering for her. And she wanted to go on the Eiffel Tower, too. A little while ago when I went to the Eiffel Tower I thought I heard her calling me. A voice just like, 'Kate! Kate!' I suppose I'm tired and I've let the thing haunt me. It couldn't have been Francesca, and yet I'm sure it was."

"You've had a tough time," said Johnnie Lambert sympathetically. "Have another drink."

"No, thank you very much."

"Then let's go out to dinner. I know we don't know each other, but we both belong to the same firm. We're both alone in Paris and we're both browned off with kids at the moment. Three good reasons. What do you say?"

"I'd like to, but I'm expecting a telephone call. I ought to wait in."

"When is this call likely to come?"

"Oh, any time."

"Give him until eight o'clock and if he hasn't phoned by then, come out with me. Fair enough?"

"Him?"

The blue, glinting eyes of Johnnie Lambert watched her humorously.

"Kate, you're much too attractive to be sitting in a Parisian hotel waiting for a girl-friend, or an elderly relative. We only have this evening, and I can show you a most intriguing little place on the Left Bank. Home by midnight. How's that?"

He was a little too hearty and masterful, but he meant to be kind. And it was quite true, an evening alone would be unendurable. How could she be sure Lucian would telephone? The answer clearly was that if he did not do so by eight o'clock he was tied up with other business or that he did not particularly want to see her again.

"All right," she said slowly.

"Fine." Johnnie's voice was full of enthusiasm. "I'll meet

you here at eight, but if you absolutely can't make it, I'll see you on the plane in the morning."

The intriguing little place that Johnnie knew was startling enough to make her temporarily forget her strange worry about Francesca, and her illogically deep disappointment that after all Lucian had not telephoned.

Johnnie Lambert had not Lucian's distinction of feature or interesting sombreness, but he was pleasant, kind and a little overpoweringly jolly. It amused him to see her reactions to the night club which flourished in the remains of a medieval dungeon. It was entered by way of a steep, winding staircase, the worn stones of which had carried feet in less happy circumstances, and the age-blackened arched ceiling of the dungeon itself was low and a little claustrophobic. Once, Johnnie told her in his hearty, untroubled voice, people had been flung in here to die. Either starvation, sickness, or the rising water of the undrained cellar carried them off. No one but the persons who occasionally flung them food, or pushed in another victim, would have heard their cries. But if their ghosts lingered, it was in a very different atmosphere of dim lights, smoke and the sound of a piano played by a middle-aged woman, with very blonde hair and very long teeth. Now and then a singer would appear to croon some low song. Once it was a man with a curious smooth face, like wax, untouched by the lines of age, yet with cold, disillusioned eyes, and later Madame herself, magnificent in black velvet, with even blacker hair, who came to roll her large, liquid eyes at her male customers.

"Do you like it?" Johnnie asked Kate.

"I'm not sure." She looked at the low ceiling, and the protruding hooks which once must have been grasped by desperate fingers. "I think of the past."

"Bless your kind heart. That's all over long ago. Water under the bridge. Dead men rise up never. That sort of thing. What shall we eat and drink? Shall I order?"

"Please do. And it is fun. But such an odd place."

Later the singers sang old French songs, "Sur le pont

d'Avignon" and "Frère Jacques." Kate hummed the melody, relaxing at last, and Johnnie, who really was very kind, leaned towards her and said, "That's better. Now you look happy. Have you stopped worrying about that kid?"

"Yes, I think so, I expect she's all right. I'll send her back her doll when we get to London."

"Tell me exactly how all this happened."

Her glass, she noticed, had been filled again. The wine and the music and the smoke and the flickering colours of the dancers' skirts were all combining to make her pleasantly fuzzy in her head. But she still had an obscure longing to be sitting in her bedroom at the hotel waiting for the telephone to ring. At this very moment, she thought, Lucian was standing somewhere, impatiently dialling the number and waiting for her to answer.

She tried, with exactitude, to recount to Johnnie the events of the journey from Rome, but her story strayed a little, and he had to keep bringing her back to the point.

"You say no one believed you had a child with you. Not even this man who helped you?"

"Lucian? But he had never seen Francesca and I hadn't talked about her. One doesn't relate all one's affairs to a stranger over dinner."

Johnnie's hand, square and soft, rested momentarily on hers.

"I wish you'd break that rule, Kate."

She looked at his face which was now very close to hers. It was too large and too red, and all its expression seemed to be in its lips. She couldn't take her eyes off those waiting lips.

Suddenly she wondered overwhelmingly why she was here, in this fusty place, its atmosphere of doom only veneered with gaiety. Why had she come? Why had she not gone to the opera, or just had a respectable early night?

It had been because Johnnie was kind, and because he worked for Mrs. Dix, which somehow made them seem to be old friends.

She made herself smile and speak lightly. "Then tell me about yourself. You have a wife and children?"

"Not me. I'm a rover. I don't like shackles. Well—depending on how decorative the shackles are. Do you know, you're very attractive. How did Mrs. Dix come to let you travel alone? Normally she's much more cautious."

"I'm competent, usually."

"I'm sure you are."

"How long have you been working with Mrs. Dix?" Kate asked.

"Five, six years. I was a schoolmaster originally, but that got too dull. I've done these odd tutoring jobs. I took an American brat, pots of money, around the world. Once I was secretary to an oil magnate, but we didn't hit it off very well. Still, this way one gets around."

The man with the wax-like face was singing again, accompanied vigorously at the piano by the lady in the mauve dress. Kate pressed her hands to her eyes and longed for fresh air. It was only eleven o'clock. Would Johnnie be hurt if she suggested leaving so early? Later, one imagined, it would be impossible to breathe in here. More people were coming down the narrow stairs, and being seated in dusky corners. Madame, large and overpowering, in her sweeping black velvet, appeared to sing "Alouetta." She was rolling her large eyes at Johnnie and he was appreciatively applauding. Kate wished she hadn't drunk so much wine. How much? Not more than two glasses. How idiotic to get so fuzzy-headed on that. She waved away the waiter who would have refilled her glass, and leaned back in her chair. Madame's voice, rich and deep, seemed to fill her head. It made it swell, made her vision a little imperfect so that the lights seemed to flicker, and Johnnie's face, nodding in time to the music, seemed far away.

"Kate"—his voice was far away, too—"are you all right?"

"I'm rather tired," she said. "I wonder if you'd mind—"

But she never finished her plea to leave, for at that moment, without warning, all the lights went out.

There was instantly a storm of voices and cries. A girl began to giggle irrepressibly. People blundered about. Madame's voice, domineering and calm, sounded above everything.

"You will please sit still. A little accident in the fusebox—in one moment it will be fixed."

"Kate, are you all right?" came Johnnie's voice very close to her ear, and he felt for her hand.

Someone began striking matches, and faces appeared phantasmagorically and disappeared. They might have been the faces of the long-ago doomed, flung in here to rot slowly. Johnnie's hand, holding hers so firmly, might have been that of a despairing fellow-prisoner. Madame suddenly appeared carrying a branched candlestick with the candles alight, and her face, large and white, floating behind it, seemed bloated and full of evil amusement.

Kate couldn't breathe. She struggled to her feet.

"Sit down!" said Johnnie. "Lights in a minute." But already she was making her way to the door. She tripped over a stool, and heard the grate of the table as Johnnie hurriedly pushed it back to follow her.

"Kate, don't panic!"

"All is well, madame. The lights in one moment. . . ."

The twisting stairway, as black as a pit, was just ahead of her. Determinedly Kate groped towards it. Uncertainly she negotiated a step. Oh, for the stars, the clean night air.

"Kate, you little idiot. Wait."

Another step. . . . And then the light shone in her face, blinding her. She moved sharply backwards and lost her balance. The other voice calling "Kate!" seemed to come out of a dream. . . .

SIX

BUT IT WAS not a dream that she was in a taxi with Lucian. She opened her eyes slowly, because for some reason her head was aching intolerably, and saw his head silhouetted against the window.

"Lucian!" she said cautiously.

He turned his head.

"Hullo," he said coolly.

"You didn't telephone."

"I couldn't earlier, and then when I did you'd gone out."

Kate tried to sit upright. Pain stabbed her head.

"How did you know where?"

"The hotel porter told me. He heard the address you gave the taxi."

"Did you follow us?"

"No."

There seemed no retort to that flat, unexplanatory answer. Kate let another street or two slide by before she said, without particular interest, "Where's Johnnie? Why am I with you?"

"Johnnie was decent enough to bow to my prior claim. Besides, he realized by then that you didn't like that particular place."

"In the dark it seemed haunted. I had to get out. I just had to." Her voice shook, as she remembered that claustrophobic horror, with the disembodied faces floating in the intermittent match-light.

"Did I behave very stupidly?" she asked, with shame.

"You gave your head a nasty bang on the stone steps. You seem to have a talent for getting into trouble."

"You frightened me, with that torch. It was you, wasn't it?"

"Coming to your rescue," he said in his detached way.

"But there wasn't really anything happening, was there? You didn't have to rescue me?"

"From a case of claustrophobia, yes. Your friend Johnnie's ideas for a gay evening didn't work out so well, did they?"

"Johnnie's all right," she said defensively. "It wasn't like going out with a stranger. He works for Mrs. Dix, too. She told him to look after me. And I really was feeling a little morbid. I kept thinking about Francesca. I thought I saw her this afternoon."

"That's absurd. Your aeroplane ticket has arrived, they told me at the desk. So catch that plane in the morning."

"I suppose so."

They had reached the hotel. Lucian paid the taxi-driver and helped her out. The soft night air swept about her face, reviving her. She wished vaguely that Lucian were not so cool and detached. He had been interested enough to find out where she had gone that evening, but only as a self-imposed duty. His manner remained aloof and rather chilling. If she were a trouble to him she wished he would go.

"Good-night, Lucian. Thank you for bringing me home."

"Better now?"

She nodded. "It was only fresh air I needed."

"And stop worrying about that child."

"I will when I know definitely where she is. I still keep thinking—"

"She's all right," he said impatiently.

"But you couldn't know that, could you? You don't even believe she exists."

He looked at her in the calculating way that was becoming a little repellent.

"Lock your door tonight," he added obscurely. "And catch that plane in the morning."

He was already going. She thought, for a dizzy moment, that all this had been imaginary.

"Why must I lock my door?"

"Foreign hotels! Here's your handbag."

"Oh, I'd forgotten it. I left it in that place."

"Yes, we found it. You need looking after, you see. All right now?"

"Yes, thank you."

"Take some aspirins. They'll fix your head. I'll see you in London, perhaps. Goodbye...."

When she reached her room the telephone was ringing. She picked it up dubiously.

"Kate? Is that you?" It was Johnnie's hearty voice, untouched by either resentment or worry.

"Yes, it's me. Where are you?"

"I'm still at this dump. The lights are working now. Sorry you seemed to get a scare. Why did you?"

"I don't know. I must be susceptible to atmosphere." She was, of course. She remembered her desolate feelings of the afternoon in the Luxembourg Gardens, the garden of the queens, with their lonely stone faces, and then the strange shivery feeling that was almost fear which had swept over her when she had thought she heard Francesca calling to her at the Eiffel Tower. Then that dungeon-like room, where one still seemed to hear doomed voices. . . . No, she was no person to cover with a veneer of gaiety the irretrievably lost and forsaken.

"Well, too bad. Rather a flop, the whole thing, eh?"

"Lucian came," she said feebly.

"You're telling me. You fell and knocked your head on the stone steps, and this character just swept me aside, saying he had the prior claim. You were his girl. Are you his girl?"

Kate remembered Lucian's cool, detached manner, and thought of William waiting in London, and sighed.

"I'm not anybody's girl."

"If I'd known that I wouldn't have behaved so decently! Well, can't be helped now. I'll see you on the plane in the morning. Just wanted to know you got home safely. So long, my dear."

The aeroplane ticket was in an envelope on her dressing-table. Kate looked at it thoughtfully. Then she picked up her handbag to count the money she had. It was a large bag. Previously to this evening there had been plenty of room to stuff even Francesca's doll into it. But before going out she had tossed the doll into her suitcase so that the bag would not bulge quite so inelegantly. Her stepmother had given her this bag a year ago, when she had been making the move to London. She had said that at a pinch it would serve for an overnight bag. It was a beautiful quality antelope, lined with silk. Kate valued it very much. In consequence it distressed her now, when she opened it, to see that the lining had got torn. There was quite a large slit in it.

She was quite sure it had not been like that before she had gone out that evening. She remembered suddenly, and with a queer, distressed feeling, Lucian saying, "You forgot your bag. We found it."

But what, in the interval before finding it, had happened?

Forcing herself to remain calm and to think, Kate searched the contents. Her passport was there, also her wallet which seemed to contain the amount of money it should. Her cosmetics were untouched, and the keys to her flat were still there. Nothing seemed to have gone. Nothing at all. Yet the lining was carefully and unobtrusively slit, as if someone had been looking for something.

It must have happened during that frightening few minutes when the lights were out. Johnnie had been sitting beside her holding her hand. He could not have held her hand and searched her bag at the same time.

It could not have been Johnnie.

But there were sundry odd people in that place. Who knew whether the lights going out had been accidental? Perhaps it was a trick that happened regularly.

But nothing had gone from her bag. No one had stolen anything, even money, which would have been quite safe and untraceable.

There had been the very short period, of course, when she had panicked and knocked herself out in the dark on the stone steps. As Lucian's torch shone in her face....

It was Lucian, apparently, who had got her into a taxi and gathered up her belongings. There would have been plenty of opportunity for him to search her bag. Plenty, indeed.

But why on earth should he? And why should he have told her to lock her door?

Abruptly the ache returned to her temples. Something was going on. Something very strange. Francesca's disappearance, the menu card that had vanished from her room while she was having her bath (because it had Lucian's face sketched on it, she realized, with sudden clarity), and now the queer happenings of this evening, that could have been caused by her own behaviour. Or her behaviour could have fitted in very nicely indeed with someone's schemes....

In a daze, Kate walked to the door and turned the key in the lock. But it was with a perfectly clear purpose that she dialled the number of the airways office.

When the clerk answered she said, "Please cancel my ticket for flight 61 in the morning. Miss Kate Tempest. No, I won't be travelling by a later plane. I'm crossing by ferry. Thank you. Good-night."

After that she had to telephone for train and steamer departure times. She would have to be at the Gare du Nord at 9 a.m., the clerk told her. But that was easy. That was the train Lucian would probably be catching, and she would be able to ask him why her handbag had been so thoroughly searched, and what he had hoped to find. She could also look for Francesca.

Something told her that the steamer she caught at Calais tomorrow would also be the steamer on which Francesca travelled to England.

For now she no longer believed that the child had been taken back to Rome. It was not so simple as that. How could it be when these mysterious things were happening to her? If her head were not aching so acutely she might have been able to think of a reason for her foolish imaginings. But just now she couldn't.

In the morning, when she had slept, she would be able to cope.

SEVEN

WHEN MRS. DIX was worried she found that her passion for chocolates, even the richest and creamiest, was not satisfying in itself. But with a dash of brandy the recipe was perfect, and she could face anything.

After Miss Squires had left for her country cottage last evening she had been alone in her over-heated, over-decorated upstairs flat, and there was no one to whom she could talk. Not that she could talk to Miss Squires very much. It wasn't wise. But at least Miss Squires knew about that poor girl in Paris, bewildered and alone. Except for the strange Englishman she had mentioned, and who was he? That was the worrying question.

Miss Squires had had the utmost faith in the girl's discretion and level-headedness, in spite of her seeming a little too attractive and lively to be over-supplied with the more mundane qualities. But Miss Squires, least of anybody, had expected this particular contretemps.

Long after Miss Squires had gone home Mrs. Dix kept having small nips of brandy interspersed with chocolates. At midnight she got out the last gift her husband had given her, a rather heavy, antique gold pendant, and clasped it around her neck, and wept a little.

Then, still sitting in her chair, a rotund little figure looking strangely young and vulnerable, she fell asleep. She slept until the first light was coming through the windows, and spasmodic footsteps and cars starting up sounded without. Then she woke with a start. The lights were still burning and she didn't at first realize it was morning. She poured another brandy and drank it quickly. Then she lifted the telephone and asked for the Hôtel Imperial in Paris.

In a short time the connection was made, and she could hear Kate Tempest's clear but slightly alarmed voice at the other end.

"It's just Mrs. Dix, dear," she said reassuringly. "Calling to see if you're all right. No more trouble, I hope."

"No, not really trouble. Just a slight mix-up."

"Mix-up?"

"Oh, with this Johnnie Lambert of yours, and the other man I met on the train, Lucian Cray. I got an awful crack on the head and Lucian took charge. But Johnnie was awfully sweet and understanding. It was nice of you to tell him to look after me."

"Me! Tell him to look after you." In spite of the warm, cushioning brandy, the fear was sweeping back, making her heart thump and the palms of her hands moist. "Who is he?"

"Johnnie Lambert. I told you. He's just back from Beirut. You remember, the tutor."

"The tutor," echoed Mrs. Dix foolishly.

"I guess you can't remember the names of all the people you get jobs for," came the girl's voice philosophically. "But he did say you had specially told him—I say, Mrs. Dix, didn't you tell him at all? Weren't you speaking to him on the phone? But in that case how did he know who I was?"

In the midst of her flurry and apprehension Mrs. Dix was sure of only one thing. Miss Squires had been wrong and she had been right. Kate Tempest had not been a suitable person to send on this job. She was too gay and ebullient, too quick to talk to strangers, and also, worst of all, too inquisitive.

"Just come home, Kate, dear," she begged. "We can talk about it then. You have your plane ticket, haven't you?"

"Yes, but I'm not using it. I'm travelling by ferry. I have a hunch, stupid, I expect, that Francesca might be on it."

"*Francesca!* What are you talking about?"

"The little girl. I don't think she's gone to Rome at all. I think someone has been playing a trick on me. I'll tell you all about it when I see you. Anyway, I enjoy a sea trip. *And* a spot of detective work. I can't face Rosita without Francesca, can I? And now I've got to rush to catch the train. Apologize to Johnnie for me if he gets home first. I'm looking forward to seeing that gentleman again."

The telephone clicked. The young, optimistic, ebullient voice vanished.

Mrs. Dix had one hand clutched to her bosom where she felt a sharp, strangulating pain. She wanted to reach for the brandy bottle to have another quick nip which would not only reassure her but despatch the pain and breathlessness.

But suddenly she felt incapable of moving. What had she done wrong? Surely yesterday, in a moment of mental aberration, she hadn't told someone to call on Kate. But if she hadn't, *who* was Johnnie Lambert?

EIGHT

IT WAS TERRIBLY disappointing. Kate had walked from end to end of the train, but there was no sign of Lucian, certainly no sign of Francesca. Her hunch about Francesca, in the broad light of day, seemed fantastic and completely unreasonable, but Lucian had told her he was travelling back to England by ferry steamer. So why was he not visible?

Feeling flat and out of temper, and with her head beginning to ache again, Kate found a seat and tried to relax. Had Mrs. Dix been annoyed with her for not using the plane ticket? She couldn't be sure, because that issue had been lost in Mrs. Dix's perplexity about Johnnie Lambert. She had sounded so uneasy and alarmed, and she said she had not spoken to any such person on the telephone. It was possible she may have had a lapse of memory—her voice had sounded fuzzy and wandering as if she were drugged or drunk. Living in her world of unreality, neither of these things would have been unexpected. But it may well have been that it was Miss Squires to whom Johnnie Lambert had spoken. It was much more likely that Miss Squires, brisk and down to earth, would suggest that Kate be looked after.

Anyway, that was unimportant. She would discover the truth when she returned to London. She was not particularly interested in Johnnie Lambert. It was Lucian whose dark, secret face both haunted and repelled her.

She should have sent a cable to William, too. He would be hurt at her neglect. But just at the moment William, too, seemed unimportant. There were only two people in her mind, the lost little girl Francesca who may badly need rescuing, and Lucian Cray who seemed to know more than he should. Otherwise why had he told her to lock her door last night?

The ferry was drearily crowded. There was the usual babel

of voices, the blue-overalled French seamen begging and exhorting the pushing and struggling passengers, the dedicated rush for possession of deck-chairs, the luggage dumped where one tripped over it, the queue for the bar and the restaurant. A cold wind blew over a choppy grey sea. Even in harbour the ship was rocking noticeably, and passengers, determined to be ill, were wearing looks of stern martyrdom.

Already Kate was realizing the foolhardiness of her plan. On a crowded ferry, with its passengers constantly moving about, what chance had she of finding one small girl. Luck would need to be with her, and she didn't at the moment feel lucky. She was remembering she had had to skip breakfast to catch the train, and now, from hunger and an aching head, and the gentle rocking, she was beginning to feel a little queasy. She decided to join the queue for coffee and sandwiches, and it was then that suddenly she saw the man with the slant-eyes and a slightly Chinese face. He was standing beside a pillar watching her. At least, his slanting eyes seemed to be fixed directly on her, because when she caught his glance it slid away. A small shock of uneasiness went through her. She didn't like being stared at so intently. And she remembered now having seen him on the Paris train when she had strolled through it looking for Lucian. He had seemed to be watching her then, too. Could it be that he was following her on this journey?

If she had caught the plane would he have been on that, too?

Nonsense, she told herself vigorously. One frequently encountered the same faces on a long journey. And it may be that this rather unsavoury-looking person found her attractive to look at.

Nevertheless, Kate had lost her appetite. She left the stuffy saloon and made her way up on deck again. They had left harbour now and were moving into a steadily increasing sea. It was going to be impossible to walk about very much, even if one's legs felt steady. Which hers suddenly didn't.

How idiotic this was, to set out on a private investigation, and be overtaken by seasickness! It was a situation that would amuse only William.

Yet it would have been rather nice if his strong arm was around her now. She had to admit that. Lucian? No, she couldn't face him at this moment....

"Kate! Kate!"

Kate started up wildly from her half doze. But among the people scattered about there was no little girl, no one had cried out. Only a seabird was circling overhead, and they were just coming into Dover harbour. The voyage was ended, and had accomplished exactly nothing but nearly two hours of misery.

Kate gritted her teeth and, gathering her possessions, forced herself into the queue so as to be one of the first ashore. From a good vantage point in the Customs shed she could make a belated watch.

Sheer determination made her succeed, and she had the satisfaction, as she stepped on to the gangway, of seeing the Chinese-looking man far down the queue. Then suddenly she saw Lucian, too. At least, it had looked like Lucian, but he was a long way back and, as Kate stared, he was lost to sight.

Kate looked helplessly at the wedged people. She hadn't a hope of pushing her way back to where she thought she had seen him. Even now she was being swept forward by impatient people behind her. Would she see him again?

Hopefully she achieved the Customs shed, and lingered near the door. The people surged in, faces of all descriptions, young, old, eager, tired, sick. Again, as if it were fated, she caught a glimpse of the sallow-faced, slant-eyed man, and immediately behind him, as if they were following him, came two men carrying a long wooden box.

That was when Kate's heart turned over in horror. It was a coffin. Surely it was a coffin. A child's. Francesca's.

A dizzy wave swept over her. She found herself blundering forward and pushing her way after the two men. They reached the desk with their burden. They put it down and waited for the Customs official. The sallow-faced man had disappeared.

Kate fought her way forward. The box had a padlock, she saw. It was really only a chest. But in horrified fascination she waited for it to be opened. The official questioned its owners. A key was produced. The lid was lifted.

It was not Francesca's composed and stolid features that lay within. It was the round, flat, white face of a grandfather clock.

The anti-climax was too much. Kate had to stifle her giggles.

"Oh, William!" she said to herself. He was the only one with whom to share this macabre joke.

But the diversion had been fatal to her plans. Now the huge room was packed with milling people, and her chance of seeing Lucian was again negligible.

She told herself disgustedly that she was about as successful as a rabbit at private investigation.

There was still, of course, the train to Victoria, and this a familiar English train in which she would not have any nightmare feeling that people were mocking her in strange languages.

She had no difficulty in getting her own baggage through Customs. Perhaps the official noticed her wan appearance and was sorry for her. He chalked her bag and handlebag with scarcely a look at them, and at last she made her way to the train.

It seemed, because of her strained and over-tired state, that she had been living on trains for months. There were the familiar piles of luggage in corridors to be climbed over, the people who impatiently let her squeeze past, the suspicious and faintly hostile look of passengers in compartments as she peered in with a murmured apology. This time she didn't ask if anyone had seen a little girl in a white dress, because it was certain Francesca would no longer be wearing the white organdie dress. In her tweed coat she would now look like any other child.

But if Kate failed instantly to recognize her, she would

recognize Kate and would cry out, as she had already done twice. Or had it been only once, at the Eiffel Tower? Or had it not been at all?

The train went smoothly and swiftly on its way, the countryside, English now, with the gentle Kentish hills and haystacks, and red-brick farmhouses, went past, the passengers chattered and dozed and consumed quantities of bread and jam and tea in the restaurant car; everyone was intent on his own business, and there was no sign of Francesca, or of Lucian, who at least should have been there.

Ironically enough, but not unexpectedly, the Chinese-looking man, with his slanted sideways glance, was the only person Kate recognized. He was not watching her now. He was standing in the corridor staring out at the passing landscape. He seemed deep in thought. He looked, Kate imagined, as if he were as disappointed as she.

Yet on the platform at Victoria Kate thought she saw Francesca. The square back of a dark-haired little girl clad in a tweed coat. Being dragged along, with apparent unwillingness, by someone Kate couldn't see in the crowd.

She began to elbow her way urgently through the jostling mob.

Strong arms swooped around her, holding her stationary. "Hey there! What's the hurry?" said William.

Kate could have slain him. "Let me go! You fool, let me go! Now I've lost her!"

"Lost who?" But William's grip had slackened and Kate had darted away.

As was to be expected, there was a queue at the barrier. When she tried to squeeze her way ahead she was glared at ferociously. She had to content herself with standing frantically on tiptoe and seeing nothing but the heads in front of her.

"Who are you looking for?" William asked mildly.

"Francesca, of course. I saw her a moment ago. At least, I think I did."

William took her arm quite gently. "Don't be a clot. She's back in Rome."

"You're saying that too!" Kate exclaimed furiously. "What do you know about it, anyway? No, don't tell me now. Thank heavens we're through the barrier at last. Wait for me at the bookstall. I've got to look for this child."

Had it been Francesca she had seen? It couldn't have been because she hadn't been on the train. At least, she hadn't seemed to be. And she wasn't now in the small, depressed-looking queue waiting for taxis. Either she was nowhere or else in Rome and Kate the victim of her own foolish obsession.

Irritably she made her way back to William.

"How did you know I would be on this train?"

"Because when you thoughtfully sent me no message of any kind, not even a postcard from the Eiffel Tower, I rang Mrs. Dix. She said you would be home alone. There had been some agonized reappraisals and the child had gone home to Poppa."

"But I don't think she has," said Kate intensely.

William took her arm. "My darling, you look remarkably like something the cat brought home. Come and have a cup of tea and tell me why you're turning this into a Hitchcock thriller."

In the café, where an overworked waitress blotted up spilt liquid from the glass-topped table, and wearily asked them what they wanted, William went on, "Mrs. Dix didn't like me phoning. She was very cagey indeed. She said you hadn't told her about me."

Kate opened her eyes which had temporarily closed. She was suddenly extraordinarily tired.

"That's true. Should I have?"

"She seemed to think so. Family background and so on."

"Oh, I told her about my stepmother. Don't be silly, you're not family." But Mrs. Dix had probed a little about friends, she remembered, and, thinking of William with whom she had just quarrelled at the time, she had dismissed the question.

"That's another thing," said William amiably. "Anyway, Mrs. Dix didn't seem overjoyed to chat with me. I wonder why?"

"I suppose you wanted to know too much. After all, she's been brought up on hush-hush stuff. Years ago her husband was in intelligence."

"Ah, that's the answer. Anyway, she did finally tell me your trip had come unstuck, and the child had been whisked back to Rome. You must have had quite a time."

Kate nodded drearily. "Seasick, too. Would you believe it? Just when I wanted to be particularly alert. And I never want to see another train in my life. Or a tourist."

The waitress had brought the tray of tea. She said, "There!" in a kind voice, as if temporarily forgetting her own troubles, whatever they were. Dirty dishes. slopped tea, sore feet. "I must look awful," thought Kate, "to take priority over those things."

She sipped the hot, strong tea and was suddenly glad William was there. Glad and grateful, but not excited. It was only William with his broad shoulders and untidy hair and penetrating gaze. Not Lucian's dark, exciting face.

"There was this Eastern-looking man all the time," she said. "I expect he was born in Bermondsey or somewhere, but he had a dash of Chinese or Malay that made him look sinister."

"When did you first see him?" William asked.

"This morning on the train. Probably he had been there all the time and I hadn't noticed him before. Though I don't see how he could have had anything to do with it, any more than Johnnie or Lucian."

"You'd better start at the beginning. And please be coherent."

Afterward, William said the only possible thing that was sinister or suspicious was her room and her handbag having been searched. But that did not necessarily need to have any connection with Francesca at all. It looked as if she had been the victim of a confidence trick perpetrated by either Johnnie or Lucian, or both of them. It was lucky she had lost nothing.

"But why did I lose nothing?" she demanded. "Confidence trick men want money. I had quite a lot of francs in my bag."

"These must have been looking for something else. They

may have picked the wrong woman, and discovered it too late. The lights going out at the joint certainly sounds like part of the plot. But I can't see that it's anything whatever to do with the child. And why you should think she's been brought to London is beyond me."

"I saw her! At least I thought I did."

"There have been scads of kids running about Victoria station."

"I heard her call me at the Eiffel Tower. I'm certain of that. Besides, who would take her back to Rome? No one there cared enough about her."

"I thought it was her father who couldn't bear to let her go."

"Him! He didn't even say goodbye to her."

"Kate! You're crying!"

Kate blinked angrily. "She was only a baby and she had on her party dress. She's been tricked and it's my fault for not looking after her properly." Kate blinked again, and the tears ran unashamedly down her cheeks. "I tell you, I won't be happy until I see her again and know she's all right."

"You're not going to Rome again?"

"I don't think I'll have to. I'm certain she's not there."

"Kate, darling, it isn't your business any longer."

"It is my business! And it isn't your business if I go straight back to Rome." Kate blew her nose, ran her fingers nervously through her hair and pushed back her chair. "Now you can take me to Mrs. Dix. She'll understand why I'm worried. On the journey it got to the stage where no one really believed there was a child at all. But Mrs. Dix knew there was. I have to talk to her."

Miss Squires was just getting ready to leave when Kate burst in. She looked up in a rather startled way, her eyes flickering behind her round, owl-like glasses.

"Why, Kate! What are you doing here at this time?"

"You know I lost Francesca, don't you? I want to see Mrs. Dix."

"Oh, dear! I don't think she'll want to be disturbed just now. We're closed, really. I'm just leaving."

"But, Miss Squires, this is urgent! It's about a lost child!"

"Not lost, Kate dear." Was there something evasive, a little uncertain, even frightened, about Miss Squires' manner? "She's been taken home."

"I'll believe that when I have proof," Kate said firmly. "Now take me up to Mrs. Dix."

"Very well. I'll see." Miss Squires was definitely flustered. Kate paced about the tiny office restlessly while she disappeared up the steep, dark stairway. Presently she came down again.

"Mrs. Dix will see you, but she's not at all pleased. She says you should have telephoned and come to see her in the morning."

"And in the meantime a child might be murdered!"

"Kate! How can you say such a thing?"

Miss Squires' eyes were suddenly enormous, her face full of uneasiness.

"I don't really mean that," Kate said quickly. "But I must be sure. Francesca wasn't exactly lovable, but she had a sort of private courage. Oh, well! I'll go up to Mrs. Dix."

Nothing had changed in the cosy, upstairs flat. Mrs. Dix wore the same brown velvet dress, and her face was pink and benign. She held out her small plump hand to Kate and then waved her to a chair. She gave no outward sign of the displeasure Miss Squires had mentioned, but she did look a little tired. Her eyes were heavy and a little glazed, and there was a strong, rather stale, smell of brandy in the room. Was brandy, as well as chocolates, one of her weaknesses?

Kate was offered the inevitable chocolate out of a particularly lush box (did a woman buy chocolates like this for herself, Kate wondered curiously), then Mrs. Dix said in her warm intimate voice, "Miss Squires tells me you're worried, my dear. But didn't I assure you none of this was your fault? If Francesca's father decided to play a trick like that—pure comic opera, I must say—none of us could help it. Rosita, although she's stricken, naturally, doesn't blame you at all. Poor Kate, you must have had a dreadful time."

"Mrs. Dix, I don't believe Francesca was taken back to Rome."

"Good gracious me! What do you believe, then?"

"That someone has brought her to London secretly for some purpose of their own. Perhaps it's to bribe her mother, or to hold her as a hostage. I don't know. But whatever it is, we've got to find that poor child."

Mrs. Dix's round soft mouth had dropped open. She was surveying Kate incredulously. "Whatever makes you say that?"

Patiently, Kate went through her reasons once more. Mrs. Dix seemed to be listening closely, but the lids had dropped slightly over her eyes, hiding their expression. And her nervous fiddling with a piece of tinfoil wrapping gave away her tension. Miss Squires had looked uneasy, too, Kate remembered.

When she had finished, however, Mrs. Dix leaned back with a relieved air.

"My dear girl, I thought you had something dreadfully sinister to tell me, but that all sounds *quite* explainable. The strange child in the bunk—such a shock for you! After that I'm sure you'd imagine you saw Francesca everywhere or heard her calling you. Someone in some book explains that kind of hallucination. It's quite common, especially after a death."

But that last word brought a sudden little silence into the room. Mrs. Dix's eyelids flew up, as if someone else had said it, and startled her, then dropped again, and she fumbled automatically for her source of comfort.

Kate watched her bite into a chocolate cream, and said rather coldly, "My things being searched was not an hallucination."

"But I told you to be careful, dear. You shouldn't trust strange men in a foreign city. Not even Johnnie Lambert who, by the way, has left a message for you. But I'm sure Johnnie would never have done a thing like that."

"You said you didn't know who he was," Kate pointed out.

"A slight mental lapse, dear." Mrs. Dix's eyes did not flicker. "I shouldn't have telephoned you so early this morning. I was only half awake, and I'd completely forgotten about talking to him the day before. He flew in this morning, very disappointed you weren't on the plane, but much more angry with me for sending him off immediately on another job. But I had an urgent mission that only he could do. He speaks Arabic, you see."

"What was the message he left?" Kate asked, much more interested in this than in the surprising information that the rather simple, hearty Johnnie Lambert could speak Arabic.

"Oh, just to tell you not to forget him, you'd be seeing him again before long. He seems to have taken quite a fancy to you." Mrs. Dix wagged her forefinger coyly. "He was terribly distressed about that little contretemps last night. The lights going out must certainly have been a planned thing, he said. He questioned several people after you'd gone, but of course one gets nowhere with that sort. However, no damage was done, thank goodness. Now tell me, please, about this other man on the train."

"He was just someone who helped me," Kate said aloofly. "He had nothing to do with Francesca's disappearance, because he was with me at the time when it must have happened. We were having dinner. I shouldn't have gone to dinner. I shouldn't have left her."

"Now, my dear, don't fret! The child's perfectly all right. I spoke to her father, the scoundrel, yesterday. I told you."

"She left her doll. She isn't happy without it."

"Have you got it with you?"

"It's here, in my handbag." Kate opened her capacious bag and took out the crushed-looking, shabby doll.

Mrs. Dix put out her hand.

"Give it to me, dear. We'll send it on to Francesca."

But Kate shook her head. She returned the doll to her bag.

"I don't think so. I'll keep it until I'm quite sure where it's to go."

Mrs. Dix was annoyed. Kate knew, by the way she picked

up a chocolate and squeezed it, smearing its liquid centre over her fingers. She made a cross little noise and wiped her fingers fastidiously.

"Really, Kate dear, I know you're tired and overstrained, but aren't you being a little exasperating. If both Francesca's parents swear she is safely back in Rome—"

"Let me speak to her on the telephone," said Kate.

"To Rome! My dear, a trunk call—"

"I'll pay for it myself."

"But the child can't speak English! You know that."

"She'll recognize my voice and I'll know hers. Please, Mrs. Dix! Put the call through. Then I'll be satisfied and I won't worry you any more. You can post the doll on to her, and we'll forget all about it."

"This is absurd!" Mrs. Dix muttered. "No one asks you to be so conscientious. Do you really insist on my doing this? I haven't time and it's most inconvenient."

"Then give me the number and I'll do it."

"No, no, that won't do at all." Mrs. Dix petulantly picked up the telephone. "Very well, if this is the only thing that will satisfy you I will put the call through. Perhaps you will join me in a brandy while we wait."

William was waiting, too, but that couldn't be helped. If she could speak to Francesca and take that dreadful weight off her mind she would go down to William and be perfectly charming to him, and not let Lucian's face come into her mind once.

Mrs. Dix tossed off her brandy very quickly, so Kate did the same. A little of the tension went out of her, but on Mrs. Dix the brandy seemed to have the opposite effect. She grew very flushed and no longer concealed her nervous glances towards the telephone. When it did ring she jumped violently, then gave a little girlish giggle and said, "I always do that. Isn't it silly!"

It took a minute or so to make the connection, and Mrs. Dix kept saying in a high voice, "I want to speak to Signor Torlini personally. No, personally, I insist. He is out? Oh, dear! Then be good enough to get his daughter to come to the telephone. His daughter! Francesca! What's that? I can't hear you! No, I don't want her nurse. Oh, you say she's in the park. The gardens? Yes, I see. They went on a little outing. Quite, quite. They won't be back for a little time yet? Oh, too bad. . . ."

Kate was leaning forward tensely, her hand out.

"Mrs. Dix, let me speak. Please!"

"No, no, it can't be helped." Mrs. Dix's high, firm voice swept on. "Thank you, thank you. No, it isn't important. Goodbye. *Arrivederci*."

She put the receiver down.

"Mrs. Dix why didn't you let me speak to whoever that was?" Kate was almost in tears from rage and frustration.

"To Antonio's secretary. That silly conceited little man! But there was no point, was there? Francesca's out. Her nurse has taken her to the Borghese Gardens. A treat, I expect, to make up for her disappointment at missing the Eiffel Tower. So we've wasted the call. Isn't that annoying. But surely it proves to you that the child is safely home and well."

"It doesn't prove anything," said Kate slowly. "How do you know whoever spoke wasn't lying?" She hadn't been able to hear what the voice on the other end had been saying. It had been a shrill gabble, a tiny, distorted, ghostly sound that seemed to her to grow more and more reiterant. It surely couldn't be that the speaker was speaking in Italian.

"Antonio's secretary lying!" Mrs. Dix exclaimed.

"Whoever he was, doesn't he know public gardens close at dark." Kate glanced out of the window. "It has been dark for over an hour, in Rome as well as in London."

Mrs. Dix drew up her stout little body haughtily.

"Miss Tempest, you're exceeding your duty—"

"I'm worried!" Kate cried. "Aren't you worried? But then you didn't see Francesca in her absurd organdie dress. She was dressed for a party, and there was no party. We just didn't manage to give her one. If you'd seen her, you wouldn't just say casually, 'She's all right.' You'd want to see her or speak to her, just to know. And that's what I intend to do, even if I have to go back to Rome to do it."

"Kate!"

"Oh, it's all right. I'm not going back immediately. First I'm going to make sure, somehow, that she isn't in London."

William was sitting with his finger gently on the horn of his car. Kate could hear the dirge on one note as she came down the stairs. She hurried, tripped slightly on the narrow steps and began to laugh as she saved herself. William was infuriating and absurd, but he had a happy knack of reducing even a nightmare to everyday proportions. She laughed again as she came out on to the street and saw him with his head stuck out of the car, in earnest conversation with a policeman, but still not stopping the monotonous dirge.

Then he saw her and grinned, and lifted his finger from the horn.

"I'm sorry, officer. I agree with all you said. But if your girl kept you waiting, especially a girl like Kate, wouldn't you do the same? Meet Kate, officer."

The policeman, very young beneath his helmet, gave a half-nod, an embarrassed grin, and moved on.

William said to Kate, "Thought you'd slipped out the back way and caught a plane back to Rome."

"No, I didn't, but we've talked to them. At least, Mrs. Dix has."

"And?"

"And Francesca at this moment is playing in the Borghese Gardens in the dark. With, I suppose, Caesar's ghost. They couldn't even think up something better than that to tell me."

"Mrs. Dix believed it?"

"She'd believe anything. She's been at the brandy bottle, and anyway she doesn't care."

William sniffed. "I'd say you'd been at the bottle, too."

Kate shivered and moved close against him. "Br-r-r. It's cold. And I've got a nightmare."

William methodically switched off all the lights and took her in his arms. She was enveloped in tweed and the scent of tobacco smoke, and she was kissed with gentle and prolonged affection. She lay quietly, feeling his exploring lips on her closed eyelids, her cheekbones and then her own lips. The sensation was agreeable, but somehow shadowy, as if it were happening to someone else. Finally William delicately lifted one of her eyelids with his fingertip.

"I told you, I've got a nightmare."

"That's what lovers are for, catching burglars and dispersing nightmares."

Kate sat up. "You're not my lover."

"Soon will be, sweetie. I keep my fingers crossed."

She wouldn't let him come in to her flat. She was going straight to bed because tomorrow she wanted to be fit and alert for what she had to do.

"Such as?" William inquired.

"First I'm going to see Rosita, Francesca's mother. If nothing comes of that I'll get another inspiration."

"Don't stick your neck out too far." For the first time William's voice was anxious. "It's really none of your business, you know."

"The welfare of a child is everybody's business," said Kate heatedly. "How can you be so callous?"

Mrs. Peebles popped out swiftly as the front door opened. "It's you," she said. "Back."

"Yes, I'm back. Any messages?"

"Not if you've seen Mr. Howard."

"You know very well I've seen him," Kate retorted. "You were looking out of the window just now."

"I wasn't looking at you and him, Miss Tempest. I was seeing if that prowler was still there."

"Prowler?"

"Someone's been strolling about rather more than necessary. I'd lock your windows tonight, if I was you."

Kate's heart missed a beat. "If he looks suspicious, why don't you call the police?"

"He doesn't look suspicious, exactly. I wouldn't have noticed him except that he had that Chinese look. That's why I remembered him the third time he passed. But he's gone now. Lor', Miss Tempest, you don't look like your holiday did you any good."

"It wasn't a holiday," Kate snapped.

"I can see that. Regular washed out, ain't you? I'd go straight to bed, if I was you. But call if you hear anyone scrabbling at the window."

"Don't be absurd, Mrs. Peebles. Who is going to scrabble? A burglar doesn't make a noise."

"Not if he's a good one. But he has to learn, doesn't he? Some of them amatoors must scrabble, by accident, anyway. Dear, oh dear, it's a sad thing my husband isn't alive. He'd have dealt with him, Chinese or not."

NINE

SO THE PROWLER, according to Mrs. Peebles, was already a burglar. Kate tried to dismiss the suggestion as absurd, but the coincidence was too strong. A Chinese-looking face, which meant he must be the man who was already her familiar, and the fact that last night in Paris her handbag had been searched. And her room, too, probably, when that sketch of Lucian had disappeared.

She had a panicky desire to ring the police and ask for protection. Or at least to summon William back. Then she told herself not to be absurd. Mrs. Peebles, a widow living alone except for the lodger in her basement, had taken exceptional care to make the house burglar-proof. All the windows had bars, and the doors double locks. No one could get in. It was perfectly safe. And, anyway, why should anyone get in? The person who had ransacked her room in Paris must have discovered that she had no valuables.

But if the man with the yellow and slant-eyed face were the same, how had he found where she lived? He had not followed her here because he had been here first.

It was more than strange. It was rather frightening. Kate put out the light and drew aside the curtain to look up on to the street. There was no one about. It was a quiet street. A cold wind and a smell of soot drifted in. She was back in London. She was safe—surely....

But as she drew her head back slow footsteps went past. She could see dark trousers, and a small, neat foot. Without leaning out and drawing attention to herself, she could not see more. As she waited, breathless, the small feet and the trousers disappeared. The footsteps died away. They did not come back.

The streets were public. Anyone was entitled to stroll down them. Kate told herself not to be foolish. If she were going to listen to every step that went past she was not going to get much sleep, and she needed sleep.

But it was odd about that prowler.

Mrs. Peebles' tap at the door made her start violently.

"I forgot these. They arrived this afternoon." She thrust a bunch of carnations into Kate's arms. Her narrow face was alive with curiosity. She knew very well that William did not send Kate carnations.

The note with them was from Johnnie Lambert.

> "In case Mrs. D. forgets to give you my message. I'm devastatingly sorry about being pushed off on another trip straight away, but I'll be seeing you—maybe sooner than you think. Love and kisses, Johnnie."

Kate said aloofly, "Thank you, Mrs. Peebles," and wondered why, for that wild moment, she had thought they might be from Lucian Cray. He did not even know her address. He had not asked for it. She wouldn't be seeing him again—ever. She hadn't even a sketch of him. She just carried his face in her mind.

It was nice of Johnnie to send her carnations. Life was always this way, William meeting her, Johnnie sending her flowers—the one with the dark, exciting face that she couldn't get out of her mind, silent.

The only face that should be in her mind was that of Francesca.

There was one more thing she could do tomorrow, if her visit to Rosita proved as unsatisfactory as had been her visit to Mrs. Dix. When Mrs. Dix had asked for the telephone number in Rome she had surreptitiously written it down. The feeling had grown on her since that Mrs. Dix and the person at the other end had been talking at cross-purposes. While someone had chattered bewilderedly in Italian, Mrs. Dix had improvised a conversation suitable for Kate's ears.

But tomorrow, if necessary, she would ring that number herself.

Now she was too tired, mentally and physically, to do anything but sleep.

It was some hours later that she was aroused by the scrabbling at the window.

No, oh, no, a burglar wouldn't make a noise like that. He would be stealthy and silent.

Kate sat up, breathing with difficulty. The windows were locked. There were bars across. She was perfectly safe.

But who was out there?

It was useless sitting here shivering. That got her nowhere. She would have to go to the window and look out. Quickly, before the would-be intruder knew he was being observed.

With resolute speed she sprang out of bed, crossed to the window and pulled back the curtain.

She found herself looking into the face of a large, black-and-white cat. It stood on the sill opening its mouth in a soundless miaou. Kate collapsed weakly.

This was all of a piece with the whole affair. The freckle-faced Annabelle sitting up in the bunk in the train, the grandfather clock with its bland white face in what she had thought had been a coffin, and now this stupid cat, pretending to be a burglar, or worse.

Perhaps everyone was right and she was turning into a nightmare something that was perfectly simple and explainable. Francesca was in Rome with her father; Lucian Cray was home from an innocent business trip; Johnnie Lambert, bored and fretful, was halfway to Arabia; Mrs. Dix was deep in a brandy-induced sleep, dreaming not of a lost child but of her lost husband; Madame and her confederates in their ghoulish nightclub in the Latin quarter were looking for another prey with a well-filled purse; the man with the Oriental face was merely looking for lodgings, or a friend's house.

And she, startled by a wandering cat, was very definitely going back to bed to sleep.

It was as well for her peace of mind that she did not notice the shadow, as long and thin as a tree, that fell across the wall, and that moved stealthily when her curtain was drawn across the window once more. Her sleep, after that, was too deep to be disturbed by the second furtive but useless testing of the very efficient bars of the window.

The sun shone the next morning. Kate got up feeling well and cheerful. When Mrs Peebles called her to the telephone she sprang up the stairs full of excited but unreasonable anticipation. Things were going to happen today. She would make them happen.

The caller was Miss Squires. "Good morning, Kate. Could you come in as soon as possible."

Was it news of Francesca? "Why?" Kate asked eagerly.

"Just a little errand. Mrs. Dix suggested you do it."

"Of course. In an hour?"

"Is that as soon as you can make it?"

"Afraid so," said Kate, keeping silent about her intended call on Rosita on the way. She was learning to be circumspect.

"Good morning, Mrs. Peebles," she called cheerfully. "I did have the scrabbler in the night. A cat."

Mrs. Peebles gasped.

"Oh, dear! Didn't you scream?"

"Almost."

"Ever so brave, aren't you?"

"Oh, I can face a cat. I'm a craven coward in real danger."

"Better keep out of it, then," said Mrs. Peebles sensibly.

It was a nice enough day to wear her grey suit. She was meeting William for lunch. She might as well look pleasant for him, as for whatever elderly client she had to meet off a train or take shopping. And also for Rosita.

She had the doll Pepita in her bag. It was Rosita who had first mentioned the doll. She would probably shed tears over it, and perhaps talk more than she would otherwise have done. In this way perhaps Kate would discover whether Francesca's mother were satisfied or happy about her child's whereabouts.

It seemed more than four days since Kate had first gone to the house in Egerton Gardens. So much had happened since she had walked up those steps to the elegant oak door with its shining brass knocker.

A woman who had been cleaning the hall opened the door. Kate thanked her and said she wanted to see Mrs. Torlini.

The woman looked puzzled.

"No one of that name lives here, Miss."

"Yes, there does. In that room at the top of the stairs. I called the other day."

"That door, Miss? That's Mrs. Thompson's room."

"Mrs. Torlini was there the other day," Kate said pleasantly. "Let me go up and see."

"You can do that, but you'll see it's Mrs. Thompson. We don't have no foreigners here.'

The thin, dark, suspicious face of the cleaning woman watched her as she went up the stairs. Can she see my heart beating? Kate wondered. Can she see the nightmare coming on again? Because of course Rosita is in that room. I *know* she is!

A completely strange, elderly woman with straggly, grey hair opened the door. She peered irritably at Kate and said, "Yes? What is it? What do you want?"

"I want Mrs. Torlini. This is her room, isn't it?"

"You've made a mistake, dear. I've been here fifteen years. You must be in the wrong house."

"But I'm not," Kate insisted earnestly. "This is the house. I remember the carpet on the stairs, and that picture. Why, I was here only four days ago, and I saw Mrs. Torlini. In this room, lying on the couch."

"Well, she's not here now," said the old woman tartly. "I've never heard of her in my life. Have a look, if you don't believe me."

Fascinated, Kate edged into the room and stared.

It was the same room. She could swear to that. There were

the long windows, the dark-red damask curtains, the numerous chairs and couches, the fireplace where she remembered it. It was the same, yet different. For it had a musty fuggy air, as if years had passed, and dust and cobwebs and an accumulation of junk had been strewn over it. A Rip Van Winkle of a room belonging to an old woman who didn't open the windows, and who kept two elderly Pekingese which came snuffling towards Kate, as bleary-eyed and suspicious as their mistress.

"But I was here," Kate protested.

"You can't have been, Miss, unless it was before 1954."

"We talked about Francesca, Mrs. Torlini's little girl. I was going to Rome to get her. Rosita was lying on that couch —no, not that one, perhaps. It looked different."

Of course it had looked different, it hadn't been covered with a shabby rug sprinkled with dog's hairs, it hadn't even been in that position facing the fireplace. Or had it?

Was she dreaming?

"You see, you are in the wrong house, dear," the old woman said. "It's easy enough to make a mistake. All these big rooms look alike. I certainly never saw you before, and neither did Mrs. Lusk. Did you, Mrs. Lusk?"

"Did I what?" called the thin, dark woman from the bottom of the stairs.

"See this young lady before?"

"Never seen her in my life."

"Rosita let me in herself that day," Kate said weakly.

"Not in here, she didn't." The old woman chuckled maliciously. "Timmy and Tommy might look harmless, but they nip the ankles of intruders. Yes, they do, don't they?" She scooped one of the over-fat, snuffling animals into her arms.

The fuggy atmosphere hit Kate afresh and her head began to swim. She must have made a mistake. It was the child in the train situation all over again, the strange, freckled face staring at her. In the same way this old woman with the straggling grey hair was not Rosita. Inexplicably, the normal bright morning had once more turned into darkness and nightmare.

But the house *was* the same one. Numbers did not change overnight, and she had this one written clearly in her diary. Besides, everything was the same about the architecture. Only that fusty room and the grotesque pair of elderly Pekes and the woman with the straggling witch-locks had been overlaid with a film of age.

Perhaps when she found Francesca she would discover that over her, too, the years had passed, and she would be a grown young woman, self-assured and independent.

Kate arrived breathlessly at the office. She swept through the outer office into Miss Squires' small, dark sanctuary.

"Miss Squires, what is Rosita's address?"

"Rosita!" Miss Squires blinked her owlish eyes. "Who is Rosita?"

"Francesca's mother, of course. Surely you know."

Did a shade come down over her eyes? Levelly she answered, "I'm afraid I don't. I never knew much about that particular mission. It was Mrs. Dix's pigeon."

But the small plump pigeon who spoke only in her own language was lost. Or stolen....

"But listen, Miss Squires. I've just called on Rosita, exactly where I interviewed her the other day, and she isn't there."

"Gone away, I expect," said Miss Squires laconically.

"Perhaps. Nothing would surprise me now. But the old woman says she has been in that particular room for fifteen years. She practically said that Rosita didn't exist. I dreamed her up, or something."

"I think you ought to mind your own business, Kate," said Miss Squires severely. "I know nothing about Rosita. I never did. But if a foreigner chooses to do a midnight flit, it isn't any business of yours, is it?"

"It's not a midnight flit," Kate persisted. "It's a sort of Rip Van Winkle thing, as if it were fifteen years since I called on her. Even the room had aged!"

Miss Squires looked at her uneasily.

"Are you sure you're all right?"

"Of course I'm all right."

"You were pretty done in yesterday. I just wondered—oh,

well, you'd better see Mrs. Dix when you come back. You can't yet. She's still resting. She had a bad night. And in the meantime there's this urgent errand to do in the city. One of our clients, an elderly lady, Mrs. Mossop, confined to her bed with arthritis, wants some gifts for her twin granddaughters' birthdays. They'll be twenty-one and she thought perhaps wrist-watches or simple gold bangles. Something tasteful, not too expensive. The jeweller she'd like you to go to is an old friend of hers. Nicolas Grundy in Hatton Garden. She said he'd help you select something."

"Must I go this morning?" Kate asked.

"I'm afraid so. Why? Don't you feel up to it?"

"Yes, I'm perfectly fit, but I had one or two things to do."

She didn't add that one of them was to put that telephone call through to the number in Rome—urgently. She was indeed learning to be circumspect, not even trusting kind, pedestrian Miss Squires.

"Can't they wait? You'll be back by midday. Mrs. Mossop wants you to take the things along to her when you've chosen them. I'll give you her address." Miss Squires smiled placatingly. "We're sending you because you have the best taste of anyone on our staff."

"Very well," said Kate reluctantly. "I'll go."

"Good girl. Oh, and by the way, Mrs. Dix asked me to see if you had Francesca's doll with you in your bag."

"Yes, I have. Why? Do you want to see it?"

"I couldn't care less about it. But the child treasures it, doesn't she? Mrs. Dix thinks it ought to be sent off at once. She told me to see about it."

Kate kept her bag firmly shut.

"Sorry, Miss Squires. This happens to be my pigeon. Francesca does treasure the doll, so I don't intend to risk her not getting it. I have to be quite sure where she is."

Miss Squires frowned in bewilderment. "But didn't Mrs. Dix explain to you that the child was with her father?"

"Oh, she explained to me, yes. She may even believe it herself. But I don't. At least, not yet. I'm waiting to be sure. And in the meantime I'm keeping the doll. Didn't you ever have something you treasured when you were a child?"

Miss Squires blinked. "Well, yes, of course. With me it was usually cats."

"And it would have mattered enormously if you lost one, and it would be up to any responsible adult to see that you got it back. Well, I feel like this about Francesca and her doll." Kate smiled. "It's not silly, it's just being decent. Now where is this place I have to go? Is Mrs. Mossop one of the talkative ones, because if so I'd better cancel my lunch date?"

"Oh, there'll be no need to do that. You'll be back in plenty of time." Miss Squires suddenly squeezed Kate's hand. "You're a nice person, Kate. Good luck."

TEN

KATE DID NOT care either for Mr. Nicolas Grundy or his shop. The latter was small, dark and very old-fashioned, and, one would imagine, barely a step away from bankruptcy. Mr. Grundy himself had beady, black eyes that gave Kate a prolonged, intent stare, a mouth suggesting craftiness, and slick, dark hair flattened over his forehead.

It was a strange place to be selected by a wealthy and no doubt fastidious old woman, but perhaps it had had past glories, and a family connection for Mrs. Mossop. Perhaps Mr. Grundy had much better wares to offer than the slightly tarnished period silver in the wall cases, or the old-fashioned rings and pendants beneath the glass counter.

However, it was still a fine, sunny morning and Kate's feeling of optimism, despite her strange experience in the house in Egerton Gardens, had returned. So she smiled pleasantly at the beady-eyed gentleman and made known her wishes.

Mr. Grundy immediately nodded with deference and understanding.

"I'll be delighted to help you. If I may say so, I know Mrs.

Mossop's tastes rather well. She's a very old customer of mine. Her taste lends itself to the austere. Something simple but good."

"These are gifts for young girls," Kate pointed out. "And I'm not to spend more than twenty pounds."

"Quite, quite. We can select something very nice for that price. What about two identical strings of cultured pearls? Or gold pendants? I have a very charming one set with topazes. That's a very fashionable stone these days."

It was true that he had better things than one would have imagined. From hidden drawers he produced turquoise brooches and rings set with amethysts or opals, and a variety of pendants. Kate spent an engrossing fifteen minutes making a choice. Finally, at Mr. Grundy's suggestion, she had several articles wrapped to take to Bloomsbury where Mrs. Mossop lived, so that the old lady might make the final selection.

Mr. Grundy directed her as to which bus to catch. For all his rather crafty and calculating appearance he had been very courteous and helpful. Kate planned to tell Mrs. Mossop so, and congratulate her on her obscure but competent jeweller.

There was something mysterious about the house of this client. Ten minutes walk from the bus stop, it was large, well-kept and obviously highly respectable. A very youthful maid answered the door and asked Kate to come in. She was taken into a large, well-furnished room overlooking the street, and asked to wait there while the maid took the package of jewellery upstairs. Mrs. Mossop couldn't come down, she explained, but Kate was to rest and take a glass of sherry.

Rather reluctantly Kate surrendered the package. She didn't know Mrs. Mossop or the two granddaughters, but it had been fun selecting pieces of jewellery, and she hoped her choice would be approved.

She refused the sherry, because she loathed drinking in the morning, but her refusal seemed to upset the maid, who was very young and nervous.

"It's poured," she said anxiously. "And biscuits."

"Very well, thank you," Kate said.

The tray with the single glass on it was brought, then the maid and the package of jewellery vanished upstairs.

Kate looked distastefully at the sherry. Good manners had made her accept it, but why should she have to drink something she didn't want, and which was probably nasty and sweet. She took a sip and her suspicion was confirmed. Sweet and syrupy. The place for that was in the bowl of chrysanthemums on the table.

No time was wasted on that small action. Then Kate sat down and relaxed, thinking with pleasure of the long, cold beer she would have when she met William.

This was a quiet street, with few people about, and only an occasional car passing. A car was parked just opposite. Its driver sat reading a newspaper, as if he were waiting for someone. Kate looked at him, thinking he might have appreciated that glass of sherry more than she had. She was a little drowsy. The strain of the last few days had not quite left her, and Mrs. Mossop was being rather a long time. The quiet of the house and the dilatoriness of her unknown employer lent itself to a five-minute nap. Almost unconsciously Kate closed her eyes.

She opened them a few minutes later and saw the face looking round the door.

A curious, disembodied face, pale and hairless, ancient and evil. It seemed to float in the air for that one horrifying moment, then, as she started up, disappeared.

There was nothing there then but the empty space beyond the partly opened door.

She could have imagined that momentary vision, except that the fear and panic that had swept over her when the lights went out in the Paris night-club now filled her again, the same urgent desire to escape. Still hardly knowing why, she was running for the door.

The jewellery, the pieces to be bought and the pieces to be returned to Mr. Grundy, were still upstairs. But that no longer mattered. There was something evil here. She must get away.

Clutching her bag, telling herself she was a hopeless coward, she hurried across the empty hall and out of the front door.

She hadn't imagined that face. Almost, out in the sunlight, she thought she had. But its uncanniness, its air of gloating, its strange sexlessness, were too vivid in her mind for imagination.

Had it been the assumedly bedridden Mrs. Mossop, spying? And how was she to explain to Mrs. Dix that she had run away in such foolish panic? How could she describe her intense sense of danger?

At the moment, none of that mattered. All that mattered was that she was in the clean, normal air again. She shivered violently as she hurried down the steps.

Then she suppressed a cry as suddenly above her a high, querulous voice called, "Wait! Wait!" She looked up swiftly, but only a shadow moved at an upstairs window, a faint, pale blur that might or might not have been that nightmare face.

Too frightened to feel shame at her panic, Kate hurried on down the street. She was vaguely aware of the small black car which had been parked opposite moving slowly forward and turning. Was someone coming out to pursue her?

Even that little maid, young and rather stupid, had been frightened. She realized that now. Why? What had been going to happen? And why was she so sure it had been going to happen to her?

There was a ten minute walk to the bus stop, a turn to the right, a crossing, and then another turn. These were quiet streets, and perhaps in her haste she was careless. She thought she had looked to her right before crossing, but, still obsessed with her strange, unreasonable panic, she hadn't noticed any traffic dangerously close, neither the car that drew up with a screech of brakes nor the small black one that swerved suddenly, catching her and sending her flying.

It was too absurd. She wasn't knocked unconscious. At least, she didn't think she had been, but when she sat up slowly, a middle-aged man was gathering up the scattered contents of her handbag, and a woman, with a little flowery hat, too youthful for her flushed, middle-aged face, was saying indignantly, "Are you all right, dear? My, that was a lucky escape. That road hog! Don't try to get up yet. My husband's got your things. Oh, and your poor nylons! Ruined! Try and see if any bones are broken."

The voice came from the other side of the Atlantic, and it was kind. Kate wanted to smile, but was aware only of an excruciating pain in her left wrist. She hugged it feebly, and fought a growing dizziness.

This really was too absurd, a bump on the head the other night, and now this, sitting in the gutter nursing an injured wrist!

"What happened?" she asked weakly.

"Why, we were innocently driving across this intersection when that little car literally shot in front of us. It had to swerve to avoid us, and hit you, poor dear."

"And didn't stop?"

"No, the bastard," came the deep, indignant voice of the man.

"Actually, Elmer, he did. He slowed right down and put his head out. But when he saw us he just hurried on."

If the driver was who she thought it was, Kate reflected, of course he wouldn't stop. For she had caught just a phantom glimpse of the Oriental face. Or had that been imagination, too?

"You poor dear, you are hurt. Elmer, we're going to take her right to the nearest hospital."

"We certainly will. And here's all your belongings, honey." The American's kind face was floating in a mist. Kate wanted to protest violently at being taken to a hospital, she couldn't spare the time, she had urgent things to do, but suddenly her mouth was stiff and she couldn't speak. She was only dimly aware of the man grinning as he held up a vague object.

"We've even rescued your kid's doll."

She wasn't badly hurt, the nurse told her. Her wrist had been sprained and was now strapped up, and she had suffered from shock. But she'd be fine by morning. Just rest and not to worry.

Kate didn't know how much later this was. To her horror she had awoken to find herself undressed and in bed. She was in a hospital ward, and outside, beyond the long windows, it was dark.

She sat up in panic. "I can't stay here. I have to go home. Why have you let me sleep like this?"

The nurse's face was young, like the little maid's in that Bloomsbury house had been, but this face did not hide fear. It was round and pleasant and carefree.

"The doctor gave you a shot of something. You needed it. Now what would you like for your supper?"

"Supper!" Kate exclaimed. "It can't be that late."

"It's six o'clock."

"But, good heavens, I had a lunch date."

"It's a little late for that, dear. If you want to send any messages that can be arranged. Now just lie down and relax."

Kate pushed back the bedclothes. "I will not relax. I'm going home."

"Oh, no, dear! You can't do that. Lie down, please. The doctor said—"

"I don't care what the doctor said. This is me, isn't it? This is my body. And all that's wrong with it is a sprained wrist. I can look after that quite well myself. So please tell the sister and bring my clothes."

She was not as strong as she had thought. And her head was full of images, faces, Francesca's lost and forlorn, the fair and ghostly ones of two Mossop granddaughters who perhaps did not even exist, who were another hallucination, the old woman in Rosita's room, with her grey straggly witch-locks, Mr. Grundy's sharp, beady eyes watching her, and last of all that indescribably evil thing from which she had fled....

"My dear child, you aren't fit to go home!" That was the firm but kind voice of the ward sister. "Have you anyone to look after you when you get there?"

"Yes," Kate lied. But it wasn't a lie, for Mrs. Peebles would flutter over her, and William, when he heard of her cowardliness, would look at her with cool, assessing eyes.

Those two people, however, would come afterwards. First she had to call on Mrs. Dix, and ask her who and what this strange new client Mrs. Mossop was, and why a man with an Oriental face seemed to be shadowing her.

These events were tied up with Francesca's disappearance. Her conclusions as to this might be illogical, but they were deeply instinctive. Just as her consciousness of danger in that house had been instinctive and unfaceable.

She *was* a coward, but she would overcome her cowardice.

She promised she would go home by taxi, and go straight to bed. The nurse who came to the door with her gave the taxi-driver her address, but as soon as they were out of sight of the hospital Kate tapped on the glass.

"Please go to Chelsea first," she instructed. "I have to make a short call."

Mrs. Dix could no longer go on stalling behind an atmosphere of cosy intimacy and generous brandies and chocolates. This time she had to make some explanations or Kate would threaten to go to the police. The police liked cut-and-dried facts, not this airy-fairy sequence of strange things that were not so much events as anticipated events. Actually, Kate could not make a charge against any single person, except the car driver for dangerous driving and he had disappeared. It would be useless to tell London police about an Italian child lost on a Continental train. She really had no story to take to the police.

But if Mrs. Dix were nervous or had a guilty conscience, the threat would alarm her.

She *had* to know about the strange transformation of Rosita's room, and that disembodied face this morning, white and hairless and indescribably menacing.

Outside Mrs. Dix's office in the narrow, dark street, off the King's Road, Kate asked the taxi-driver to wait.

She would be too late to see Miss Squires, who must surely be wondering why she hadn't reported back that afternoon, but a light showed behind the drawn curtains in Mrs. Dix's upstairs room. Knowing she, at least, was in, Kate pressed the bell and waited.

No one came. She listened for the slow footsteps that would herald Mrs. Dix's approach down the narrow staircase. There was no sound from within.

Kate pushed the bell again, and felt the door move slightly. It hadn't been latched properly. Goodness, Mrs. Dix was no doubt comfortably upstairs having her fourth or fifth brandy, unaware that her offices downstairs could be entered and robbed.

In some nervousness, which was not helped by her aching wrist or her annoying feeling of weakness, Kate pushed the door completely open and stepped over the dark threshold.

She couldn't find the light switch. She groped across the small, outer office, feeling for it, but instead came to the door leading to Miss Squires' office and the stairway. There would be a light at the foot of the stairs, if she could find it.

She could see something white glimmering on the floor. It looked like the plaster head of a child that had used to stand on the stairpost, a rather haunting piece of sculpture with wild locks and an empty lost stare.

Someone must have knocked it down. She stepped aside to avoid it and her foot encountered something else, a large, soft obstacle, a sack of clothes, surely.

She groped with her uninjured hand. Her fingers encountered something cool, pallid.

Her heart stopped, then jerked into a sickening beat. She tried to get to her feet, but could do nothing but sit there calling in a high, unrecognizable voice, "Help! Help!"

Afterwards she could only remember the taxi-driver saying, "Gawd!" She didn't notice him go to the telephone and ring for the police.

He had found the light switch and she wished he hadn't. For now she could see Mrs. Dix's forlorn, upturned face, her body round and bloated in the brown velvet dress.

She sat on the edge of the stairs shivering, until two policemen came, brisk and seemingly unperturbed.

One of them rang for a doctor and an ambulance. The other asked her some brief questions.

Looked as if the lady had fallen down the stairs, he said. Regular death-trap they looked, too, for a woman of her build. Did she suffer from heart trouble? If so, the explanation was simple. Someone had rung the bell and she had hurried down to answer it, but had unfortunately not reached the door alive.

"The door wasn't quite latched," Kate said tonelessly. "If there were someone there, he didn't know how easy it was to get in."

"That was careless," said the constable. "I'd have discovered it on my rounds later, of course. But too late."

Too late indeed, Kate thought, looking with her shocked, exhausted eyes at the chocolate meringue figure lying so still on the floor, the cosy, evasive little person who had never quite told her the truth. And now never would.

As she stumbled into her room at long last, brought home in the police car, and equipped with a sedative given her by the police doctor, a long figure detached itself from the armchair.

"What are you doing here?" she asked crossly.

"Waiting. Waiting since lunchtime for a message or an apology which I was optimistic enough to expect.

"Oh, William, I hadn't a chance. I'm sorry. Too much—just too much—happens."

Her voice was slurring curiously. William crossed the room. "Kate, have you been drinking?"

Brandy. That was what the police had said. They had gone upstairs and found, in Mrs. Dix's warm, brightly-lit room, an empty brandy bottle, a half-filled glass, and an overturned box of chocolates, which indicated that she had sprung up hastily to answer the doorbell. She had not only been tipsy, she had also suffered from a weak heart. A bad fall would be fatal to her, and the dark, steep stairs, and her own unsteady condition, had provided that. There were no marks of violence on her body, and no immediate evidence that anyone else had been in the room, though that would be checked more thoroughly. Kate had been told to go home and get a good rest and not to worry. But also to stay in London as she would probably be required to give evidence at the inquest.

That was all. She had wanted a cut-and-dried fact to present to the police, and now there was one. But it was going to answer exactly nothing.

"Yes, I've just had some brandy," she answered William. "That nice constable gave it to me." She began to shudder. "Ugh! I loathe brandy."

William had switched on another light, and was looking at her properly. "What have you done to yourself? You look as if you've been in a fight."

Kate nursed her wrist. "I survived. Mrs. Dix—Mrs. Dix—" The words wouldn't come out. She looked at William piteously.

"Kate, darling! Tell me. Has something happened to Mrs. Dix?"

She nodded. "The stairs. A death-trap, the police said. And she drinks too much. I didn't know—about the drinking, I mean—until last night. I suppose, with a husband one perpetually grieves over, one gets driven to it. There was this plaster cast of a child's head knocked down beside her. It seemed symbolic, somehow—lost-looking, like Francesca. And those two Mossop granddaughters who probably don't exist. And that diabolical face—they're all hallucinations, every one of them! Excuse me, William. I think I'm going to be sick."

When she came back from the bathroom she was quite calm again.

"Sorry about that," she said matter-of-factly. "I suppose I should have stayed in the hospital. But I'll be all right now."

William was methodically putting the kettle on. He looked up sharply. "The hospital?" His face was a mixture of disbelief and concern, almost comical. "Well, never mind. Tell me later. I'm making some tea. Go and get straight into bed."

"Yes, in a moment—"

"Now."

"I want to make a telephone call first. I'll have to go and see Mrs. Peebles."

"Kate, you can do your telephoning in the morning."

"This I can't. I have to know."

Mrs. Peebles gasped and looked nervous when Kate said she wanted to put a call through to Rome.

"Goodness, will this instrument be good enough?"

"Of course it will. It works, doesn't it?" She didn't need to check the number she had scribbled down in Mrs. Dix's flat last night. It was graven on her mind. The operator said the call would take a little while to come through. In the interval Kate sat in the hall, unable now to move away from the telephone that was presently either going to answer her question or baffle her further.

Mrs. Peebles had noticed her appearance and was staring inquisitively.

"You had an accident, Miss Tempest?"

William had come up the stairs, so Kate, supporting her injured wrist, told them briefly about the speeding car. She didn't add her quite unprovable belief that the driver had been the man with the slant eyes and yellowish face.

"It wasn't serious," she said flatly, "and the Americans were awfully kind. I'd be perfectly all right now if—"

She stopped. She hadn't told Mrs. Peebles about Mrs. Dix. At this moment she couldn't stand the woman's sharp-faced curiosity. She remained silent, and presently felt William's hand on her head. The gesture was meant to be sympathetic and reassuring, but William had a large, heavy hand. It was almost insupportable. She felt like Atlas, with the world on her head, and moved crossly away.

"Don't do that."

"All right, angel. You've got a lot more to tell us. What you were doing in Bloomsbury, for instance."

"Oh, a job. Have you noticed that—that person today, Mrs. Peebles?"

"Who do you mean? The prowler? The scrabbler? No, I haven't seen him, thank goodness. Anyway, you said it was a cat."

"It was, too." Prowler. . . . Scrabbler. . . . Both words came out of the nightmare. Kate felt sick again, and when the telephone suddenly rang she jumped convulsively.

A perfectly unintelligible voice answered hers. She realized someone was speaking in the rapid Italian which sounded so excited and inflammatory. Probably he was merely saying, "Who is it, please?" but the sentence went on for a very long time. At last Kate was able to say slowly, "Is there anyone there who speaks English? *Parla inglese?*"

There came another long, excitable statement. Kate gave a little despairing sound. William came over and took the receiver from her.

"What is it you want to say?" he inquired laconically.

"Ask him who is speaking and what that number belongs to."

William, in what appeared to be fluent Italian, spoke for a few moments.

Then he turned to Kate, his eyebrows raised.

"Do you want to speak to the night watchman at a cardboard box factory?"

"Is that who it is?"

"That's what he says."

"Oh, my God, I suspected she was making up that call last night. Now I know, and it's too late. I can't ask her why she did it. I can't ask her anything—" The bleak knowledge swept over her. She pressed her hands to her eyes. "Now we'll never know," she said hopelessly.

ELEVEN

WILLIAM STAYED THE night. He carried Kate down the basement stairs and put her to bed.

Helping her to undress he hurt her injured wrist, and she exclaimed with tears in her eyes, "Oh, you're so clumsy! I hate you."

"Get into bed and stop talking." He jerked the bedclothes straight and grinned down at her significantly. "It will be a different story when you're well."

"It will be no story at all. And I'm not ill."

But the tears continued to run down her face, and even they did not shut out the constant picture of Mrs. Dix's upturned face, and the plump, twisted body in its brown velvet dress. Like a fat chocolate slightly squashed out of its healthy rotundity.

The simile was grotesque and made Kate begin to sob audibly.

"Your sedative," said William professionally, bringing her two tablets and a glass of water.

"Will I have to go to the inquest?"

"I expect so. But that won't be for a day or two."

"I can't face it. I'm such a coward. I ran away from that face this morning. I just ran away. I couldn't stop myself. This sensation of awful fear comes over me. It did at the night-club in Paris, too." She looked up bleakly. "I despise myself."

William sat on the side of the bed and looked at her reflectively. Her pale face had shrunken by shock and illness to childish proportions, her dark hair was mussed, her eyes tragic. She was impetuous and reckless and tenderhearted, and sometimes deliberately obtuse and maddening, and just now quite plain to look at, but still completely irresistible.

He told her so, in a detached way, and added, "I don't care how cowardly you are. Looking after you is my job. You just have to do the loving."

"Who?" she asked suspiciously.

"You could start with me. After that we'll think of lost children, and poor, foolish old women who stuff themselves with too much sugar and liquor and trip on stairs."

"Do you think that's what happened?"

"I don't know the set-up, but would anyone want to murder her and commit no theft?"

"It might have been so that she couldn't tell the truth about Francesca."

William looked at her and gave a short laugh. "Darling

Kate, your one-track mind astonishes me. Of all the incredible things you've told me tonight, that is the most fantastic. Now forget it. Take your pills and go to sleep. I'll be in the next room."

Kate sat up. "You will not. What will Mrs. Peebles say?"

"Mrs. Peebles has given me her blessing. She said something about not letting a cat in if it scrabbled. I won't let anything in. Now lie down and go to sleep."

"Oh, go away."

But half an hour later, in a shamed voice, trying in vain to shake off her drugged, haunted half-sleep, she called to him.

"William!"

"Yes. What's the matter?"

He was at the doorway, filling it with his bulk.

"You haven't got any pyjamas," she said irrelevantly.

"I don't usually bring an overnight bag. What's the matter? Can't you sleep?"

He stood beside her. She was hot and restless, and her head felt as if it were bursting. There had been so many confusing, terrifying things. She couldn't rest. She couldn't sleep. Nothing was real any more and she wanted to die.

"What's the matter, Kate? Shall I leave the light on?"

She nodded. "I'm such a coward. I should have stayed this morning. I might have found out something."

"Something that wouldn't have been your business."

"Oh, don't be so good-mannered!" she said wildly. "The time is past for behaving politely. I should have gone up the stairs and demanded to see that old woman with her non-existent granddaughters. I should have found out about that nightmare face. I should have frightened Mrs. Thompson until she confessed about Rosita, who *did* live in that room, I know. I should have insisted on Mrs. Dix"—she closed her eyes miserably—"or is Mrs. Dix meant to be a horrible example to me."

"Just stop talking," said William. "I'll hold your hand. There. Now go to sleep."

Strangely enough, she did. And woke in the morning, in a mood of cool, exhausted sanity, to see William sprawled awkwardly against her bed, his hand slipped from her grasp, his head buried in the blankets.

Dear William, she thought. But he shouldn't have spent the night here. Mrs. Peebles, for all her flap last night, was not going to approve, and Mrs. Peebles, in a disapproving mood, was tiresome. She sulked, and got secretive about telephone messages. Besides, one hadn't been as ill as that. Or had one?

It seemed one had, for when, after drinking the coffee which William had made with surprising efficiency, she tried to get up, her legs collapsed like a stuffed doll's. She was furious with herself and then more furious with William when he announced he was going.

"And leaving me to die!" she cried indignantly.

"I have to shave," he said mildly. "And go to the office and do one or two other things. Besides, I've got an infernal crick in my neck. You might give a thought to that."

"I didn't ask you to sit by my bed all night."

"I didn't intend to. I fell asleep." He rubbed his neck ruefully. Then he swooped over her with his overpowering virility. "You're not too fragile to be kissed, are you?"

His unshaven face scratched her. His hands beneath her shoulders lifted her, and jarred her sore wrist. She wanted to be angry, then, all at once, couldn't be. For, for the first time, Mrs. Dix's dead face vanished from before her eyes. In a curious and irresistible way life flowed back into her. She couldn't think of anything else but the wonderful exhilarating fact that she was alive, alive....

"Well," said William gruffly, "that was better."

He came back some time later. He hadn't yet been to the office, he said. As far as that was concerned, his secretary had been told he was suffering from acute fibrositis. But he had taken it on himself to call at the house in Bloomsbury, on the pretext that Kate had been worried about the jewellery she had not returned to Mr. Grundy. There he had seen not only the small, gauche maid, but the old lady herself.

"Because you're a man!" Kate cried in disgust. "These horrid, conceited old women!"

"She was in an invalid's chair," William said. "She was very old, but quite harmless, as far as I could see. She said she'd chosen the pearl necklaces, and sent the rest of the stuff back to Mr. Grundy herself. She wanted to know if you'd been taken ill yesterday."

"I was," Kate said bleakly. "I told you. With cowardice."

William ignored that. He went on, "There didn't seem to be anyone else living in the house, but of course I couldn't pry into every room. I had a glass of sherry—"

"Was it all right?"

"Sweet and nasty. Did you think it was drugged?"

"It could have been," Kate muttered, the shadow of her strange fear touching her again.

"Well, it wasn't. For me, anyway. But old ladies like me. I heard a lot of very dull family history, and finally came away. Then I called on Mr. Nicholas Grundy, and asked if he had any French clocks, Louis XIV, which was the only period I was interested in. But he hadn't, which didn't surprise me, in that rather scruffy shop."

Kate began to giggle. "What an absurd detective you would make! What conclusions did you come to?"

"If anything, that Mr. Grundy knew his stuff too well to run such an obscure business. But then he may have a mind above money."

"Not with those beady eyes!"

"That sounds like your famous intuition again," William said sceptically. And you know what that gets you."

"What did you do then?"

"I went to see Miss Squires. But she wasn't there. The office was closed."

"Then she's down at her cottage. And all alone, poor thing. I must go and see her."

"She'll be up for the funeral. You can see her then."

Kate winced. "Must I go—to the funeral?"

William took her hand in his. "I think so, darling. I want to come with you."

"Oh, I understand. To see who's there?"
"Ostensibly to support you." He patted her hand briskly. "I also saw the police."
"Oh—"
"The inquest is tomorrow. They're not proposing to call you unless the coroner insists. They don't think he will. It's a straightforward case of death by misadventure. There were no fingerprints, nothing."
"The door was unlatched."
"Apparently Miss Squires says Mrs. Dix was sometimes a little careless about that. She would go out late to shop, and not always pull it properly shut behind her. The inference is, of course, her uncertain condition. She hit the brandy bottle rather heavily."
Kate leaned back on her pillows. "So there's nothing. Absolutely nothing."
"Nothing at all."
She gazed bleakly at the ceiling. Then she picked up her sketching pad from the bed and flung it angrily on the floor.
"I've sketched Nicolas Grundy and the woman in Rosita's room from memory, but I can't do that face I saw at Mrs. Mossop's. There's nothing in my memory. Just a feeling. As if it had been projected into my mind. Can you understand?"
"An hallucination," said William calmly, picking up the pad and looking at the sketches she had done. A little later he added, "But the Mossop granddaughters weren't an hallucination. I saw their photographs. Smug creatures who'll grow into stout matrons. Not like you."
"No," said Kate, nursing her wrist. "If I keep on like this I won't have a chance to."

It seemed a very long time, that morning two days later, since she had walked blithely into the small, poor-looking house in the outer suburbs of Rome to collect a little girl dressed in a white party frock. Who would have guessed the anticipated party would be a funeral? At least, this was one thing Francesca was spared. One hoped that somewhere she was innocently and happily pursuing childhood pleasures.

To shut out the forlorn scene in the churchyard, Kate conjured up a picture of Francesca, plump and stolid, splashing happily on the fringe of some blue Italian lake, or eating her way through a large plateful of ravioli in a good restaurant, or even being taken on a shopping expedition to buy a replacement for poor, shabby, lost Pepita.

Coming to the funeral was a gesture of respect for her late employer, but as far as solving any of the problems was concerned, it was a waste of time. For, strangely enough, not even Miss Squires was there. Nor anyone else whom Kate would have recognized. She looked in vain for Rosita, the grey-haired woman who now lived in Rosita's room, even Johnnie Lambert, who might conceivably have been back in London.

Among the seven or eight people, all of whom looked like elderly relatives, either of Mrs. Dix or the late major, there was no familiar face.

Death by misadventure. The coroner had not hesitated to give his verdict. For what semblance of suspicion was there that Mrs. Dix might have met a more violent death?

If, by any long chance, the mystery surrounding Francesca had put Mrs. Dix in danger, Miss Squires would have mentioned it. But Miss Squires, surprisingly, was absent,

Kate listened, stony-faced, to the completion of the service, then slipped her hand into William's arm and whispered, "Let's go."

William helped her into the car. It was her first day out and she was still a little shaky.

"Well," he said. "End of story."

"End of the chapter only."

"Then I don't know where the next instalment is coming from. Nothing could have been more conventional or innocent than that little gathering."

"One doesn't expect intrigue at a funeral."

"No, but one does rather expect one's fellow intriguers to pay their last respects. Even a gangster achieves that recognition."

"I think we expected too much," said Kate sensibly. "I

had hoped Rosita, at least, might have been there. But she wasn't. What do you have to do now?"

"Take you home and go to the office."

"You couldn't take the afternoon off, could you?"

William beamed at her. "Darling, that's perfectly sweet of you, but—"

"I'm only using you." Kate said, with her usual honesty. "I want to go down to Sussex to see Miss Squires."

"In that case I'm much too busy. I've got an editorial hanging over me, and Saunders is away with 'flu. I really shouldn't have taken time off to come out here."

"Then I'll have to go by train."

William stopped the car and turned to her. His face was serious.

"Kate, you've got to drop this thing. As far as you're concerned, it's over, and I don't want you ever to go near that office again. You've finished with your old women's shopping and your poodle-minding. If you need a job I'll find you one. Or you could marry me. But you're not going back to that place any more."

Kate's chin went up.

"Or I could take a Green Line bus," she reflected. "That would actually drop me nearer to the cottage."

"Kate, look here! You've already had two peculiar accidents through inquisitiveness, and I don't like it. If there's anything wrong it's nothing to do with us. So let's drop it and carry on as we were."

Kate's forced calmness deserted her.

"How can anything ever be the same again?" she flared. "Every time I see a little girl in a white dress I'll think of Francesca and how I let her down. All my life this will go on, and it's no use your saying: 'Nonsense, you'll forget!' because I won't. I've got to find her, William. She may be ill. She may be dead. At the very least she may be unhappy and bewildered and frightened. If ever I'm to have peace of mind again I've got to find her."

William looked at her for a long time.

"And so you propose looking for her in the depths of Sussex."

"Not for her. For a clue."

William shrugged fatalistically, and started the engine.

"All right, which road do we take?"

"The Kingston by-pass. Darling, you are sweet."

"Save your honeyed words for Miss Squires."

Kate snuggled against him. "What's your editorial on?"

"The state of the roads."

"How perfectly splendid. You can get some local colour this afternoon. So it needn't be entirely wasted for you, after all."

"My dearest angel," said William, with detached vehemence, "in a very short time I am going to take to beating you."

Beneath her facetiousness, Kate was very glad that William had come. This was her first day out since her accident, and she was ridiculously nervous. She didn't think she could have gone anywhere alone, without all the time looking over her shoulder to see whether the Chinese-faced man had suddenly appeared, like a rabbit out of a magician's hat. If she had travelled on a bus she would have seen him two seats behind her, or he would have been the ticket collector, and as for a train, it was inevitable that he would have been strolling up and down the corridor, never looking at her directly, but always conscious of her.

But he would not be likely to follow William, who was a fast driver, into the heart of Sussex. She relaxed, almost contentedly, and thought of the long talk she would have with Miss Squires in the privacy of her country cottage. With no eavesdropper, Miss Squires would tell her all she knew. For what point now was there in concealing anything?

At first it didn't seem as if anyone were home. The cottage stood behind a high yew hedge which, when Kate had passed through the gate, concealed the car. She had refused to allow William to come with her, fearing that in front of him Miss Squires might refuse to talk. But now, as she stood on the doorstep, she was tempted to call to him. It was growing dark, and the trees and bushes rustled with the country wind. Also, it was strange that although no lights showed Kate had the uncanny, prickly feeling that someone was peeping at her through the blank windows.

She rang the bell again, then rapped.

At last a sound, oddly cautious, came from within. It was almost as if Miss Squires were tiptoeing to the door. Goodness, if she were as nervous as that she shouldn't live alone in the country.

The door opened a little, then wider, as Miss Squires realized who her caller was.

"Kate!" she exclaimed.

"Hullo, can I come in? I want to talk to you."

Miss Squires backed a step away down the dark hall. Oddly, even now, she had not put a light on. Kate realized that she was hugging her black-and-white cat, Tom, who struggled in her arms.

"Yes, come in," she said nervously. "I wasn't expecting anyone. Tom and I were sitting here alone. I thought you were ill."

"I had a slight mishap. I'm better now."

"Mishap?" Miss Squires' eyes, seeming doubly large in the gloom, stared at her. Really, it was as if one had trapped a wild shy owl in this little, dark cottage.

"Oh, just a fall. I sprained my wrist."

"Shut the door, please," begged Miss Squires.

"I'm sorry. It is cold, isn't it?"

"It's not the cold. I don't want Tom to go out. He might—" she hesitated almost imperceptibly, "stray."

Kate followed her square, shortish figure into the little living-room that looked over the back garden. The last time Kate had visited here, this room had been a cheerful place, full of sunlight, gay with chintzes, and Miss Squires' favourite flower reprints. But in the chilly autumn gloom all the colour had drained out of it. It was shadowy, box-like, claustrophobic.

"Do you like sitting in the dark?" Kate tried to speak lightly. Miss Squires hadn't gone to Mrs. Dix's funeral, yet all the gloom of the funeral was here. And something else, a feeling of fear, as if, now that she was indoors, the watching eyes were outside, trying to look in.

"I was sitting thinking. I'll put the light on. No, let me draw the curtains first."

She did this rapidly, as if she, too, were conscious of the eyes and the rustle in the syringa bushes.

"There," she said, as she switched the light on. She was still hugging the cat. Her face was quite colourless, Kate noticed, her eyes enormous. "Sit down, Kate. How nice to see you."

"You weren't at the office and you weren't at the funeral. I wanted to talk to you."

"Yes?" The flat monosyllable was not encouraging, and utterly unlike Miss Squires.

"This has been a dreadful shock to you."

"It was you who found her."

"I know. But she wasn't my friend, as she must have been yours. You must have known her very well—I mean, whether this sort of thing was likely to happen."

"It was very likely to happen. I'd begged her for years to have a companion, or a maid. I knew her heart was bad, and she'd got—careless."

Miss Squires didn't look at Kate as she said this. She sounded as if she were reciting a set piece. It was what she had told the police, of course, and no doubt repeated over and over to banish her own self-reproach. She sat squarely in her chair, nursing the heavy cat, hugging him as if she were afraid someone were going to snatch him from her. He was not a particularly attractive cat, being too fat and with a permanently angry expression. He hardly looked a worthy recipient for the possessive love he received. The whole thing was extremely pathetic, the dark, quiet little house, and this lonely woman clinging to her cat.

There was a short silence. Miss Squires made an obvious effort.

"You didn't come all this way alone?"

"No, William drove me. He's outside."

"Oh ! Won't he come in—"

"No, please. I wanted to see you alone."

"Alone?" There was no mistaking now the dark alarm in the woman's eyes.

Kate began to speak rapidly. "I know you will think I'm crazy, as William said everyone else does, but what do you know about Francesca? You do know something, don't you? Please tell me."

"That wretched child!" Miss Squires exclaimed. "You haven't come all the way down here about her?"

"Yes, I have. Because I can't get rid of the feeling that Mrs. Dix's death is something to do with her."

"Stuff and nonsense!" But there was a faint shine of perspiration on Miss Squires' brow. And it was cold in this room. Very cold.

"You know where she is, don't you? She isn't at that place in Rome, because I checked the telephone number. Mrs. Dix made it up, for some extraordinary reason. So where is she, and why is she hidden?"

"I know nothing," said Miss Squires loudly. "I can't think why you imagine I should."

"But why has Rosita disappeared, and why does that man follow me? You *must* know something."

"Nothing! Nothing, nothing!"

The cat, alarmed, struggled afresh in Miss Squires' arms. She held on to it and licked her lips, trying to smile, her eyes ashamed.

"I'm sorry, Kate. I'm upset. I still can't believe Mrs. Dix is—dead. And then—"

"Then what?"

"Oh, nothing."

"What?" Kate persisted impatiently.

"Oh, just one of those coincidences. Bad news never comes singly. One of my neighbours is a bird watcher and he can't stand Tom. He wrote me a letter saying he was putting out poison. So now I can't let Tom out of my sight."

"Oh, Miss Squires, how awful! You poor thing, you can't stay here alone."

"I can stay here. No one will make me move. No one will drive me away."

And sit hour after hour holding that great cat, afraid to let it out of her grasp, afraid that the warm life would go out of it, too....

"Then couldn't you get someone to stay with you?"

"Why?"

"Because it really is rather lonely." Kate's voice faltered as she encountered the suddenly inimical stare.

"I like it like this. It was perfect until lately."

"Everything is going wrong for everybody," Kate burst out. "As if there's a blight. Perhaps I am crazy, thinking it started with Francesca. But everything—Rosita disappearing, me being knocked down, Mrs. Dix dying—even Johnnie Lambert being sent away so quickly. He'd only just got home. You must know about that."

"I've never heard of Johnnie Lambert."

"But you must have!"

Miss Squires didn't look up this time. Her eyelids remained over her disturbing eyes. She said in a low voice, "I can tell you nothing, Kate. You've wasted your time. I'm sorry. But it's no use your asking me."

"I think you do know," said Kate slowly. "You won't tell."

"Nothing!" repeated Miss Squires on a rising note. She must have squeezed the cat, for he gave a bad-tempered grumble. "I'm just staying here quietly alone to get over the shock. So please—don't bother me."

Kate stood up miserably. Then, impulsively, she crossed the room and kissed Miss Squires on the cheek. "I wish you could have helped me."

Miss Squires shook her head. There were tears in her eyes. Her mouth trembled violently. "I'm sorry. I'm sorry."

In the cool darkness Kate climbed into the car beside William.

"Will you stop at the next house, please. I just want a word with Mrs. Wallace. She's a nice little thing. Miss Squires likes her. Or used to."

It was only to ask Mrs. Wallace to keep an eye on Miss Squires, about whom Kate was now acutely worried.

"She thinks someone is going to poison her cat," she explained.

Mrs. Wallace was astonished.

"But who would poison Tom. We're all silly about him. Even Colonel Maitland, who adores his birds. But he wouldn't lift a finger to hurt Tom."

"I think she's a little unbalanced," Kate said. "Her employer died suddenly. It's been an awful shock to her."

"Don't you worry, dear. We'll keep an eye on her," the woman promised.

That was all Kate could do. The trip had been useless as far as getting any information was concerned. Indeed, it had added to her heavy sense of worry, for the memory of Miss Squires sitting hugging her cat was going to haunt her.

She told William all there was to tell, then laid her head against his arm and closed her eyes. Without speaking again, they followed the long road back to London.

TWELVE

"YOU DIDN'T TELL me that gentleman was coming to look at the furniture," Mrs. Peebles complained, as Kate came in.

Kate stopped dead. "What gentleman? What furniture?"

"It was the bow-fronted tallboy he was particularly interested in. And you'd told him I'd let him in."

"Did you?" Kate breathed.

Mrs. Peebles nodded. "I didn't know what to do, frankly. But I thought if I stood over him it would be all right. So I did. Breathed down his neck." She gave a harsh dry chuckle.

"And he looked at the tallboy?"

"Oh, yes. Opened every drawer. Mussed among your things a bit, but said he had to see if the mahogany was genuine, or something. Then he seemed disappointed, and said he was afraid it wouldn't interest him. He wondered if you had any other pieces you wanted to sell."

"That tallboy belonged to my great-grandmother," said Kate dispassionately. "I haven't the slightest intention of selling it."

Mrs. Peebles' mouth took on its familiar expression that was comically like a fish gasping for air.

"You mean you didn't ask him to come?"

"I asked no one to come, and I thought you'd have more sense than to let a complete stranger in."

"But he said—I mean he looked so respectable—"

"Not Chinese?"

"You mean the prowler? Oh, no! I wouldn't have been daft enough to let someone like that in. No, this gentleman came from the city, I should think. A bowler hat, and an umbrella. He was short and dark. Had very sharp little eyes."

"Beady eyes?" Kate asked breathlessly.

"You could call them that."

Mr. Grundy. Nicolas Grundy. The jeweller from Hatton Garden. Could it have been him? And if so, why?

Kate was deeply perturbed. She began to walk away.

"I'm sorry, Miss Tempest, if I did the wrong thing."

"I don't suppose any harm has been done." It might have prevented a forced entry during the night, which would have frightened her out of her wits, and perhaps ended with her following Mrs. Dix. . . . Kate fought her fear. "Just don't do it again," she said.

But now one fact, at least, had become clear, and she must have been moronic not to have thought of it before. She had something which somebody badly wanted. That would account for the Oriental shadow, for her room being searched in Paris, for the accident with the swerving car, even for that horrid face that had hung momentarily in the air at Mrs. Mossop's. For if the caller today had been Nicolas Grundy, then he, too, was in the plot, and also the unseen Mrs. Mossop.

That glass of sherry must have been drugged, and someone had been waiting for her to fall asleep. Therefore, whatever it was they wanted must be something she would probably be carrying on her person, or in her handbag.

But also something that at times she might leave behind, so that, given any possible opportunity, her room would be searched....

A jeweller suggested jewels.

She had no jewels of any great value. And she had never been shadowed like this before. It had begun only with her trip to Rome and getting Francesca.... Francesca! The extra thing she carried about was Francesca's doll. And that had seemed to interest both Mrs. Dix and Miss Squires. Mrs. Dix had begged to have possession of it. Rosita, at the very beginning, had specially mentioned it. In Rome, Gianetta had reminded them to take it.

Kate flew to her bed where she had, not very originally, hidden the doll under the mattress. Usually she had carried it with her in her large handbag, but this morning she had remembered the American waving it at her in the road the other day, and she had decided it was foolish to carry it about with her. Besides, she had taken a smaller handbag. Someone must have been watching, and seen her leave the house with the smaller bag.

But Mrs. Peebles, with her threatening, battle-axe manner, had blocked their rather bungling attempt to search the room.

All this went through Kate's head as she held up the smallish, battered doll and studied it. It was very light. It must be hollow. But if it were stuffed with anything, it would not be particularly light.

Was she imagining the whole thing? She twisted the doll's head and arms, but all were firmly attached. Then she tore the dress off, exposing its rotund stomach. Ah! There was sticking plaster around the middle, stuck on clumsily.

With trembling fingers Kate stripped it, and there was the crack around the doll's middle, faint but unmistakable. It screwed in half.

It took only a few seconds to take it apart.

But there was no miniature Jonah hiding inside its interior, only a folded and much-creased piece of paper.

Kate unfolded it and found it was half of a letter, and it was written obviously to Francesca. It began,

"Hullo, little one,

Get Gianetta to turn this into your own language for you. I am coming to Rome at the beginning of next week and want to see you. Wear your party dress and I'll take you out to tea. Tony and Caroline send their love, and long to see you. Soon perhaps they will. Remember what I told you. Not a word—

And that was all. The last half, no doubt through much creasing, had been torn off, so there was no signature, no clue as to what it was the writer wished Francesca to remember. Nor who the writer was.

The date was two months earlier, and the address a street in St. John's Wood, London.

Kate tried to keep calm and make deductions. The letter was something Francesca had treasured, as proof its careful hiding place. It had been written by someone English, living in London, of whom Francesca was extremely fond. The casual address sounded as if the writer were a man. The vigorous handwriting had a masculine look. There was no doubt the writer was sharing a secret with Francesca. The unfinished sentence "Not a word" was obviously an instruction not to tell anyone either of the letter or of the unknown's imminent arrival.

It might have been done because it was a prank that appealed to Francesca's sober little heart, but it might have had much deeper implications. Even then, it might have been a plot to kidnap the child....

Did this explain Francesca's stubborn determination to wear her party frock when she set out on the journey with Kate? Had she expected then to meet this unknown person? Kate was suddenly remembering her excitement in the train when she had tried to tell Kate of her brief mysterious conversation with a man.

Now she was realizing Mrs. Dix's shrewdness in selecting a courier for Francesca who could not speak Italian. Francesca might have had too many secrets to give away.

Did Mrs. Dix know of this mysterious person who wrote

affectionate letters to the Italian child? Or was it to find some evidence, such as this letter, that Kate herself had been followed, and her room broken into?

There was no doubt now that it was possession of the doll that had been desired.

Who knew she had had it? Lucian Cray, Johnnie Lambert, Mrs. Dix, Miss Squires. . . . No one else, except people who might have been informed by one of these. Nicolas Grundy, for instance, and Mrs. Mossop. The Chinese-faced man. The old woman in Rosita's room.

Everything was still a mystery, but there was one practical thing that could be done at once. She could pay a surprise visit to the house in St. John's Wood and see who lived there.

At the thought of doing this, a cold, heavy stone of fear settled in Kate's heart. She tried to think of many valid reasons for not going. She had promised William not to go out again tonight—the matter of Francesca, whether it be a bitter quarrel between the divorced parents, or something more dangerous, was none of her affair—if the child were in trouble, she could not be of any help if she were lured into a strange house and knocked on the head.

But there was no use in arguing with herself. She knew she was going. With all the aplomb she could muster she was once more going to thrust herself uninvited into l'affaire Francesca. And this time, she told herself firmly, no happening, however frightening or grotesque, would induce her to run away.

After she had pressed the bell of the strange house in vain, and then rapped the heavy knocker against the door, Kate stepped back, almost in tears from disappointment. Because now that the house in St. John's Wood seemed to be empty, she had forgotten possible danger, and was conscious only of frustration.

Was this hopeful clue only proving to be another blind alley?

One of the tall windows on the second floor shot up. A vague, stout form leaned out.

"It's no use your knocking down there, young lady. There's no one home."

Kate looked up eagerly. "Do you know when they'll be back?"

"Afraid I don't. She took the children down into the country after her husband died. To her mother's, I suppose. She didn't talk much to anybody. Just passed the time of day if we met on the stairs. And that wasn't often, because I mostly use the side entrance." Belatedly, the old woman, for Kate could discern her halo of white hair now, asked, "Are you a friend of hers?"

"No. It was another matter."

The cool night wind blew the unswept leaves on the steps with a melancholy rustling. Kate looked at the long, blank windows, and had a sensation, not of fear, but of intense sadness. Where were the mysterious woman and children who had lived here, and who was the husband who had died?

"Would you like to come up, dear, and have a glass of sherry?"

The garrulous voice above her may have been purely kind. But Kate was thinking illogically of another old woman, unseen but queerly menacing. Mrs. Mossop.

"That's very kind of you, but I won't. I'll call again."

"Well, I can't say when they'll be home, dear. Before long, I expect, as there's the children's schooling. Caroline was going to a school near here, and the boy—"

"Tony?" Kate broke in.

"Yes, Tony. His mother was taking him to a kindergarten each afternoon. A bright little scamp, the dead spit of his father. Gracious, when that news came—"

"Did the father die unexpectedly?"

"Very suddenly," replied the old woman, with macabre relish. "Drowned."

Kate drew in her breath. "How?"

"No one seems to know, dear. They say it was an accident. But those foreigners will say anything."

"Foreigners?"

"Oh, yes, it was in a nasty foreign river. The Tiber."

Kate grasped the iron railings. She thought that her voice, considering the difficulty with which she spoke, was very cunning.

"What did you say his name was?"

"Lor' bless me, didn't you know who you were calling on? It's the Crays. Poor souls!"

Kate took two sleeping tablets that night, and as a consequence seemed to be struggling all night with the cold muddy waters of the Tiber. She awoke feeling limp and with a sensation of horror still hanging over her. It was at that psychological moment that the letter came.

It had been addressed to her care of Mrs. Dix's office, and had been re-addressed. The postmark was "Roma." The letter inside was written in stilted English.

"Dear Miss Tempest,

You were so kind to the little bambina Francesca. It will be of sorrow to you to hear she is in trouble. She needs a friend. There is only you of whom I know to write. Can you give help?

Gianetta."

The voice of Kate's stepmother at the other end of the wire was full of surprise and pleasure.

"Kate darling! Are you coming down?"

"Yes, tomorrow, if I may. But only if you can do something for me, Stella."

"Anything, my dear. Anything. And I've masses of vegetables and flowers and fresh eggs for you to take back to town. I'd been going to write to you. Did you know I won the prize with the largest pumpkin? And that new chrysanthemum is a great success. Everyone wants cuttings. What a pity you can't grow a slip in a pot. What is it you want, dear? A piece of furniture? Come and take your pick. It's really yours, just as much as it is mine."

"It's not furniture, Stella. It's money. I have to take an unexpected trip to Rome."

"How exciting! Is it a holiday, or for that odd woman you work for?"

Her stepmother was the most incurious of people. She accepted everything, except a heavy frost that blackened her garden, with equanimity. Nevertheless, one couldn't remotely tell her the truth—that the trip to Rome was to look for a lost child and to find out the reason for a man being drowned in the Tiber. The horror of that last was too recent to be able to talk of it at all.

"A little of each, Stella. I have twenty pounds, but I'll need perhaps another thirty. I'll travel second-class, and I'll pay you back as soon as I possibly can."

"Nonsense, darling! Don't talk of paying back. Haven't I always told you that everything your father left me is yours, too. Come down early tomorrow and we'll have a long day in the garden. I want your opinion on my new rose bed."

She had promised William to do nothing without telling him first. But already the promise was broken. For he would never have allowed her to do this. He would have said she was mad. Perhaps she was mad. Certainly she couldn't reason intelligently. But now she knew, as her intuition had told her all along, that Francesca was in trouble. And in addition there was the tragedy of Lucian Cray. Why should he, who had merely given her friendly assistance on the train, be dragged dead from the Tiber?

She hadn't really fallen in love with him, she told herself passionately. It had only been that his face, sombre, dark and exciting, with more than a hint of ruthlessness, had stayed persistently in her mind. She hadn't visualized him with a wife and children. Neither had she believed he was merely putting on a very clever act when he had helped her look for Francesca.

For if he had written that letter to the child, then he was very deeply implicated. So deeply, that the dirty turgid water of the Tiber had claimed him....

She was growing as cunning as everyone else. She packed her bag, and told Mrs. Peebles she was going to stay with her stepmother in Dorset for a few days. Then, because her memory played her a trick and she was suddenly remembering that kiss of William's the other morning, when, sore and aching and exhausted, she had had that moment of strange ecstasy, she rang William.

And found it one of the hardest things she had ever done to lie to him.

But he wouldn't have let her go if he knew the truth. He would even lock her in her room, if necessary. She remembered his overpowering strength which was not always curbed by gentleness, and shuddered with that strange, wry pleasure.

"How are the roads of England?" she asked lightly.

"In a lamentable state. Hullo, darling, I was just going to call you. Aren't you up early?" His deep, lazy voice hid his concern. "Has anything happened?"

"No. I've just decided to go down and see Stella for a day or two."

When she heard the relief in his voice she was full of shame.

"Jolly good idea. I'd have suggested it myself if I'd thought you'd listen to my suggestions."

"William, I always do."

"Yes, and then kick them out the door. Well, never mind. Have a nice horticultural time. I'll come down in a day or so, if I may."

"Not until the weekend. Stella and I will be busy, and so will you, for that matter. I guess the magazine likes to see its editor once in a way."

There was a brief silence. She knew he was biting on his pipe. She could see his shaggy eyebrows, and the reflective look in his eyes. She visualized his big body slumped comfortably in the leather armchair in which he always worked, his untidy hair, his square, strong hand gripping the telephone. She had a sudden, lost, dismayed feeling that all of that, too, was vulnerable, as had been Lucian's finer, slighter body and dedicated face.

She was a low, contriving, dishonourable person, and it

would be only what she deserved if she never saw William again.

But the thought made her catch her breath.

"Kate—are you all right?" With his uncanny and exasperating intuition he had caught her mood.

"Yes, I'm all right. I'm in rude health, considering everything."

"Your wrist better?"

"I've taken the bandage off. It's almost normal."

"Get Stella to massage it for you. And don't go trying to pull up hefty weeds, such as thistles. Or mandrake roots."

"They're supposed to cry out."

"Then I promise you I'll hear them and come to the rescue."

Now she had three clear days. Stella, at the weekend, would tell William where she was. But by then she hoped she would be cabling that Francesca was found and that all her alarms had signified nothing.

THIRTEEN

MRS. PEEBLES WAS distrustful by nature. Until she was proved definitely wrong, she regarded all strangers with suspicion. One had to, living in London, and having all and sundry coming to one's door. Besides, strange things had been happening lately. More than once she had had the feeling that the house was being watched, though not again by that slinky little foreigner with the yellow face. It was just a feeling, one might say, with nothing to substantiate it but the rather odd way Miss Tempest had been behaving, the dreadful accident that had happened to her employer, not to mention cats scrabbling at the window in the night, and yesterday that smug little man who had said, as cool as could be, that he had been instructed to come and value Miss Tempest's furniture. Her suspicious nature had served her well then, for if she had left him alone in the flat what would have been missing one couldn't guess. As it was, there had been an uncanny moment when he had glared at her with his little, hard, black eyes.

The queer thing about that was that Miss Tempest didn't have valuables. She was a nice girl, obviously well brought up, but she was as poor as a church mouse. So what she could have that would interest a burglar, goodness only knew.

With these events behind her, it was natural that Mrs. Peebles should look with even greater suspicion at the little square woman with the large round glasses who rang her doorbell soon after Miss Tempest had left for the country.

Glasses. A disguise, of course. Though this was no bold person inveigling her way in, but a strangely timid and frightened-looking woman who got out of a taxi and who carried a wicker cat basket.

Mrs. Peebles had no fear of being unable to cope with this caller.

"What do you want?" she asked uncompromisingly.

"Is Miss Tempest in? She does live here, doesn't she?"

"She does, but she's away. Left yesterday." (And no doubt you know it already, my good woman!)

"Oh dear! What shall I do now? Where has she gone, do you mind telling me?"

Mrs. Peebles was beginning to change her mind about this visitor. She seemed to be genuinely upset about something, and she also looked dead beat, standing there holding that basket that contained a now vociferous animal. No one with felonious intent would be fool enough to hamper herself with a cat while on the way to do the dark deed.

So she saw no reason for concealing Miss Tempest's whereabouts.

"She's gone down to her stepmother in Dorset for a few days. She needed a rest, poor dear. Looking downright peaky, she was."

The person on the doorstep came closer, thrusting her spectacled face up at Mrs. Peebles appealingly.

"Are you sure? Are you really sure that's where she's gone?"

"I didn't follow her to the train," Mrs. Peebles said tartly. "But I don't see why she should make it up? Why should she?"

"That's another thing," the woman muttered. "Oh dear. It's terribly important that I should see her. And it would take me so long to get to Dorset. Besides, Tom hates travelling."

Mrs. Peebles didn't quite know what to do. She said the first thing that came into her head.

"Why don't you go and see Mr. Howard. That's Miss Tempest's boyfriend. He'll know more than me, most likely. And anyway, he's a man." Mrs. Peebles looked wistful as she paid this tribute to the opposite sex. If her husband had been alive he would have known how to deal with these strange callers. It pleased her to forget that in his lifetime he had let most decisions rest on her own tough little shoulders.

"His office is in Fleet Street," she said. "Wait and I'll get the number for you."

So that was how Miss Squires came to be sitting in William's office, occupying the big, low, leather armchair, while Tom squawked grumblingly in the cat basket at her feet, and William, unable for once to relax, walked up and down, frowning thoughtfully.

"What makes you think Kate isn't at her stepmother's at all?"

"Because I'm afraid they'll get her away. Probably back to Rome."

"Rome!"

"That's the most likely place. That's where she thinks the child is."

"But *why*, Miss Squires?"

"I tell you, I don't know. I don't really know anything except that I know too much, if you understand what I mean."

William nodded. The incomprehensible sentence made sense to him. He understood that much. Miss Squires was the inadvertent possessor of a little dangerous knowledge. Hence the threat she had received by telephone that if she should divulge anything at all, or make any suspicious moves, she would receive due punishment. The first thing that would happen would be that her cat would have a mysterious accident, or disappear.

And all that had happened was that Miss Squires had discovered that Mrs. Dix's husband, the long-lost major, had come home. She had left the office one evening but, on her way to Victoria station, had found she had forgotten Tom's fish, so had gone back. The street door, in Mrs. Dix's careless way, had not been quite latched and she had gone in quietly. But there had been a light on the stairs, and from above she had heard voices raised.

"You're telling me you won't do it? But of course you will. You will be my obedient wife, as always...."

Then there had been silence, and Miss Squires, overcome by some strange revulsion, had fled.

The voice, she said, had been pleasant enough, but the words had opened up a vista of possibilities that had filled her with alarm and apprehension. She had finally persuaded herself she must have imagined the conversation, but had plucked up courage to mention the matter lightly to Mrs. Dix the next day.

"I must have been having hallucinations last night. I forgot Tom's fish and came back for it, and I thought I heard someone upstairs saying he was your husband."

Mrs. Dix's eyes, she said, had been so stricken that she had been ashamed she had raised the subject. For Mrs. Dix swore she had been completely alone, as she always was, and what Miss Squires had heard had been merely a play on the radio. Mrs. Dix had it turned on loudly, because after she had had two or three drinks she didn't seem to hear so well....

But in spite of being ashamed of her foolish imagination, Miss Squires had been extremely perturbed when Kate kept on worrying about that lost child, and then when Mrs. Dix had died she had been quite terrified. For, before the police had come down to her cottage to question her as to her employer's habits, the telephone call had come, the low, menacing voice telling her what would happen to Tom, her precious and only living possession, if she should tell anything at all that she may have discovered, or think she had discovered.

So she had been too cowardly to talk to Kate the other night. And now she was terribly sorry.

William stopped pacing up and down, and put his pipe aside.

"You've had quite a time, haven't you," he said kindly. "Would you like some tea? I'll get my secretary to make it. While she's doing that I'll ring Kate in Dorset. That will settle that matter."

It was Kate's stepmother who answered the telephone.

"You want Kate. Oh, is that you, William? But Kate's not here. She left to catch the ferry last night."

"Where to?" William asked sharply.

"She was on her way to Rome. Didn't she tell you? What's the matter with her, William? She was in the strangest mood. Couldn't settle to anything. Didn't even notice my new chrysanthemum that I'm particularly proud of. It won the prize—what's that, dear?"

"Did she tell you where she was planning to stay in Rome?"

"Oh, no, not a clue. She was completely vague. Said she was looking for a face to sketch. What *was* she talking about?"

"She's doing a rogue's gallery," said William. "Look, I must go now."

"William, Kate isn't running away from you, is she?"

"My God, no! She'd better not be."

"So it is true," said Miss Squires, looking up at William with her sad, owlish gaze.

"I'm afraid so."

"What will you do?"

"Follow her. What hotel did she stay at when she was last there?"

"The Romano."

"That's the first clue. She will probably go back there. Now listen, here's what you have to do. Don't attempt to go back to your cottage at present. Go to my flat. I'll give you the keys. No, I'll take you myself. It's not luxurious, but you'll be all right there for a day or two. My housekeeper will look after you. I'll tell her you're doing a research job for me. And she adores cats." William knelt to put his finger playfully in Tom's basket. He withdrew it hurriedly and sucked it.

For the first time a glimmer of a smile appeared on Miss Squires' worried face.

"He's very naughty. He hates that basket. Mr. Howard, you're being awfully kind. I can't thank you enough."

"Not at all," he said absently. "It's you who ought to be thanked. We'll do that later. Kate and I," he added.

FOURTEEN

AT THE HOTEL they remembered her. This was the first pleasant thing that had happened since the commencement of her long journey.

"Miss Tempest! How nice to see you back so soon," the dark-eyed clerk said in impeccable English, and a little of Kate's tiredness and frowstiness melted away.

"I'm afraid I haven't booked."

"No matter. It is the off season. The tourists go home. You would like your old room?"

"Yes, please. If I may."

"But certainly. You will be staying a long time?" The dark, liquid eyes rested on her with genuine pleasure.

"No, not a long time. Probably just a day or two. It depends on some business I have to do."

"Ah, signorina! There are better things to do in Rome than business."

"I absolutely agree. But it can't be helped."

The high-ceilinged room on the third floor, the circle of red carpet making a brilliant pool in the middle of the bare floor, the brass knobs on the bed, the wardrobe big enough to hide in. And if one stuck one's head far enough out of the window, the view of the via Vittoria Veneto, with its side-walk cafés, gay umbrellas and acacia trees.

Kate had the momentary illusion that nothing of the last fortnight had happened. She had arrived in Rome to get Francesca, and nothing would go wrong. They would reach London safely; Mrs. Dix would welcome them, smiling her cosy smile and offering them chocolates; Rosita would be waiting eagerly to receive her daughter; there would be no tragic body of the young man, who had cast his exciting shadow momentarily over her life, fished out of the Tiber....

If only this were so. If only she could be gay and carefree. But instead of bathing and resting, and then strolling down the via Veneto enjoying the late afternoon sunshine, still warm and golden, she must now set her mind at rest by going at once to the house off the Appian Way to see Gianetta.

Once again, like a repeat scene in a badly edited film, she took a taxi and asked the driver to wait. The house, in the narrow, poor street, seemed even more squalid than she remembered it. Again she was conscious of eyes behind the dark windows of the houses on both sides. A taxi would not often come down this street. It would be a matter of great interest and suspicion, perhaps, when it did.

She had to wait a few moments after knocking on the door. It flashed through her mind that she seemed to have been spending a lot of time over the last few days knocking on doors and wondering, with this sick beat to her heart, who would appear. Supposing, as in Rosita's room, a completely strange person opened this door?

But, no. It was Gianetta. She remembered the thin, dark woman in her faded cotton dress very well. She was overjoyed that for once the right person stood before her.

"Gianetta!" she cried, holding out her hand.

But the woman moved back a step, her dark eyes flickering from Kate to the taxi, and then back to Kate again. There was no recognition on her face.

"You remember me! Kate Tempest from London. I came to get Francesca."

The woman shook her head slowly. Her face was tight with suspicion.

"*Mi perdoni*, signorina." Then she added in her careful English, "I do not remember ever seeing you before. Why have you come here?"

"But I came to get Francesca!" Kate cried. "Less than two weeks ago. You must remember me. Or if you don't you certainly know Francesca."

"Francesca? Who is she?"

Kate had a moment of complete unreality. Was she really standing here before the door of a shabby Italian house, while its tenant backed farther into the darkness of the small rooms behind the open door. Rather frantically she searched in her bag.

"Look, Gianetta, you're simply telling lies. Here's your letter saying you were worried about Francesca. Now what about that?"

The woman took a quick, suspicious glance at the sheet of paper, then she peered closer.

Her head came up, and this time there was no doubting her sincerity.

"It's written in *Inglese*. I cannot write *Inglese*. What does it say?"

"Gianetta, you're not telling the truth. You speak English, you must write it."

"No, no. I only learn to speak, not to write. My husband taught me when he lived. He was a bookseller."

"But here's your name at the bottom. Signed Gianetta."

The woman's eyes flicked down at the sheet of paper, then up again. She had her thin, brown hands clasped tightly against her breast. There was fear in her face, distinct fear.

"I did not write it, signorina. I tell you truthfully."

It almost seemed that she was speaking the truth. But the fear in her eyes made Kate's heart turn cold.

"Then if you didn't write this letter, Gianetta, you still must know something about Francesca. You're her nurse, after all. Is she really with her father, and is she all right?"

"You keep saying this name, Francesca. I tell you I do not

know who you talk about. You must have come to the wrong house, signorina. Letters I do not write, women I do not know."

Her voice was growing bolder now, and rather angry. But the fear had been there. Kate hadn't imagined the fear.

"Francesca isn't a woman, she's a child. She wore a white dress and a blue bow in her hair. She had her doll, Pepita." It seemed she had made this description hundreds of times, and no one had really listened to her or believed her. "Of course you know who Francesca is."

The woman shook her head stubbornly.

"And you I have never seen in my life before. You say I lie. It is you who lie, signorina. I ask you to go."

"But I waited in that room!" Kate protested. "I can tell you exactly what you have in it, a table, three chairs, some rush matting on the floor, a plaster statuette of the Virgin above the door—"

The woman gave a faint smile. "You are saying what is in every house on this street. Knock at all the doors and ask for this Francesca. Someone may know what you want. But not me. *Scusi*, signorina, I am busy, I must go."

She was shutting the door. "Gianetta!" Kate cried in despair. "I'm trying to help Francesca. This letter says she needs help. And it has your name on it."

"There is more than one Gianetta in Rome, signorina. Go and find another one who can help you. It is not me. I know nothing that you talk about."

The door slammed in her face.

The taxi-driver was grinning at her sympathetically. He did not speak English so could not have understood what was said, but he knew she had been snubbed. How much worse than snubbed, fortunately, he could not know. For apart from the fact that Gianetta had been most deliberately and outrageously lying when she denied any knowledge of Francesca, it really seemed that she may not have written the letter. And if she had not written it, who had? Was Francesca really in trouble, or had the letter been a trick to get her, Kate, to Rome?

Because Rome was an easier place than London in which to do strange things to English citizens. It would matter, but not too greatly, if the body of a foreigner were found in the Tiber....

She got back into the taxi and told the driver to take her back to her hotel. He backed to the corner and turned with a flourish, in a fast circle that threw Kate against the upholstery and even caused the blasé Italian pedestrian, used to the fast and furious driving of motorized vehicles, to look around.

It was then that Kate caught a glimpse of the yellow watchful face beneath the pulled-down hat brim.

Well, there was her shadow back again. She almost waved him a friendly greeting. She hoped he was a good traveller, or he may have cursed this inconvenient and unexpected journey to Rome. But of course it would not have been unexpected. He had probably known about it before she had known herself.

The letter must have been a trick. Gianetta must have been lying to a certain extent—it *couldn't* have been an hallucination that she had gone there to get Francesca, the rather stout, solemn child in the party frock—but she had not been lying about the letter. Kate was almost certain of that.

So someone else had written it. Who? And why?

She sat in her hotel room pondering the next step. There was an obvious one. To look up the Torlinis in the telephone book and ring them all, one by one.

Or go to see them.

But the thought of more inhospitable doorsteps leading into strange and hostile houses made her flinch. Suddenly she wished she had told William of this impetuous journey. She could have telephoned him from Dover just before the boat sailed. He could not have stopped her at that stage, and if he didn't in thorough exasperation wash his hands of her altogether he might conceivably have caught a plane to Rome. She would not have been afraid to stand on hostile doorsteps if he were beside her. Belatedly, she was realizing that.

The light was dying. The sky was primrose and the evening mild. If it were not for the Torlinis and their mysterious child she could have gone on a leisurely tour of the fountains, or sat in a café on the via Vittoria Veneto sketching the faces of the passers-by, the priests in their brown habits and Biblical sandals, the street urchins, large-eyed, barefoot and cheerful, the old women in their narrow, economical, black dresses, the laughing young girls with their boy friends. . . .

Reluctantly, because of the mild, lemon-coloured evening, not because of her apprehension, she picked up the telephone book.

At the same moment footsteps came down the corridor. They stopped outside her door. There was a brisk knock.

"Come in," Kate said, startled.

The door opened. And Johnnie Lambert was saying in his hearty voice, "Surprise, surprise!"

"Johnnie!"

"So we meet again. How are you, darling? Did you get my flowers the other day?"

"Yes, I did. It was sweet of you."

"Mrs. Dix, the slave driver, didn't give me a chance to be home for five minutes. You were partly responsible for that."

"Me?"

"Yes, with that kid you lost. But let's talk about that later. I say, it's grand to see you again. After you walking out on me in Paris and cancelling your air ticket. When I saw your name in the register downstairs I couldn't believe my eyes. They said you got in this afternoon. I've just arrived back from Florence. Couldn't have a nicer welcome than finding you. Let's go and have a drink."

He was looking ridiculously pleased to see her. His round, highly coloured face beamed with pleasure. In his tweed jacket, with his ruddy cheeks, pale blue eyes and carefully cut hair he looked very English and familiar. Kate realized she was almost as pleased to see him as he was her.

"I'd love to," she said. "And if you're here about Francesca you're going to save me a lot of trouble. But why didn't Mrs. Dix tell me she had sent you here?"

"And the moment I'd got back to London, confound her! She didn't want to worry you. She said you were in enough of a flap already and the kidnapping, or whatever it was, hadn't been your fault."

Kate hesitated. "You knew Mrs. Dix was dead?"

Johnnie's face sobered. "Yes, poor old girl. They cabled me. Jolly bad show. I'd have come straight home, but I thought the wisest thing was to settle this child business first, if possible. After all, those had been her last instructions to me."

"And you have settled it?" Kate asked, with intense interest.

"Not a bit of it. Quite frankly, I'm no further ahead than when I arrived. I got a clue that the kid might be in Florence, so I hared off there yesterday, but no luck."

"And I went to see Gianetta, the nurse, this afternoon. She absolutely denied ever having heard of Francesca."

Johnnie nodded perplexedly.

"I know. That's what I've met with all the time. Blank faces. Who's Francesca Torlini? Dash it all, I can't even trace her father. I've called on every Torlini in Rome. The whole thing seems to be one enormous myth. Is there anything at all to prove the kid really does exist?"

"Yes, her doll."

"Did you bring it with you?"

"It's here."

Kate took the much-travelled, shabby doll out of her bag and handed it to Johnnie. He studied it casually.

"Nothing particularly ravishing about this. It feels light. Is it hollow?"

"It comes in half. I discovered that quite accidentally. Francesca had used it to keep her love letters in."

"Love letters!"

"Oh, just a rather incomprehensible note from someone in London. Someone who was apparently expecting to see her quite soon."

"Who?" Johnnie asked.

"There was no name. It had been torn off. I did call at the address, but there was no one home. Only the woman who lived in the flat above, and she said the house belonged to Lucian Cray. You remember, the man in Paris."

"Ah! Indeed! So he wasn't so innocent after all, by jove."

"Apparently not," Kate said miserably. "Because the woman said he was dead."

"Dead!"

Kate nodded. "Drowned in the Tiber."

"Here! Just recently!" Johnnie was horrified. "The plot thickens."

"He must have come straight back to look for Francesca. He'd pretended on the train not to know her, but he must have, if he wrote that letter. And there was the man she was trying to tell me about who had talked to her on the train. She seemed very excited and pleased. It must have been him."

"But, Kate, this is terrible!"

Kate nodded again and began to weep a little, remembering Lucian's dark, sombre face with which, for a while, she had imagined herself falling in love. Johnnie put his arm around her in a comforting way.

"Poor Kate, you have taken this to heart, haven't you? You shouldn't have come back here, you know. I'd no idea the thing was as serious as this. I wonder what the racket is. One thing, I'll bet that wily old fox, Mrs. Dix, knew."

"Do you think her death might not have been accidental?"

"Well, that's another thing." He gave her a quick hug, and said, "Look here, let's skip it for a while and have a little relaxation."

"How can we skip it?"

Johnnie had picked up the doll, and lifting its clothing discovered the way its body pulled in half. Thoughtfully he peered into the empty interior.

"Well, there we are. A doll with an empty stomach and Francesca disappeared into thin air. I know what it is, the deuced doll has eaten her, eh? Dash it, I've worked hard this week, and it's wonderful to see you again. Of course, we can take an evening off."

"And go to another doubtful night-club?"

Johnnie grinned apologetically.

"That was a bad show. Something queer going on that night. I'm terribly sorry about it. No, I wasn't planning to go night-clubbing. I thought I'd take you to see some people I know, after dinner. They live a little way out in the Alban Hills. We could drive out and be back by midnight."

"Oh, no, Johnnie. Thank you very much. But I've come here to find Francesca and I can't waste time. Did you say you had called on all the Torlinis?"

"Well, actually," Johnnie admitted, "I wasn't entirely skipping business tonight. These people I want to take you to are Torlinis. They say they don't know anything, but I had a feeling they were hedging a bit. I think you might get them to talk, or you might put two and two together. Women's intuition and what not. Frankly, I haven't a clue what else to do. We're up a blind alley."

"Why didn't you tell me who these people were?"

Johnnie looked wistful. "I'd have been more flattered if you'd just wanted to come with me. Not with this confounded kid's ghost between us."

"Oh, Johnnie! You are silly."

His eyes swept over her, rather lingeringly. "And you're—well, never mind. How long will it take you to get ready?"

"Ten minutes. I'll meet you downstairs."

"Right. I'll have martinis laid on."

Now she was happier and her immediate fear had gone. Good old Johnnie, not the world's most perspicacious private detective, with his open face and his hearty voice, but at least a well-meaning one. Although the plot seemed to thicken ominously it no longer seemed so sinister. It would be difficult for anything to seem sinister in Johnnie's cheerful presence. With his support they might even make a vital discovery this evening.

Alert with anticipation, Kate washed and changed her dress. She was just about to leave her room when the telephone rang.

Impatiently she answered it. Then her fingers tightened around the receiver and she was rigid.

"Kate, is that you? This is Lucian Cray."

"*Lucian!*" she exclaimed disbelievingly.

"I've just got a moment. Will you listen quickly?" His voice was rapid and breathless. The connection, also, was bad, and the sounds distorted. It seemed like Lucian, but he was dead, drowned. How could she be sure this was Lucian speaking?

"Francesca is in England. She's with—" A whirring and clicking obscured what he said. Then his voice came clear again. "—and Caroline and Tony. You must go home at once. You should never have come here. Will you go home?"

Kate found her voice sufficiently to protest. "She can't be in England. I had a letter saying she needed help here. Who sent me that letter?"

The connection was very bad. There was a roaring and clicking. The voice was more distorted and almost unintelligible.

"—Somerset, just outside Taunton." Then the words, "Letter was a hoax," came clearly, and, "Go home, you interfering little fool! It's not safe here for you."

That was all. The telephone clicked and the speaker, whoever he had been, was gone.

Kate sped down the stairs.

"Hey, have you seen a ghost?" Johnnie asked, getting up from the table in the lounge.

Breathlessly she told him what had happened.

"He said he was Lucian. But the old woman told me he was drowned. Is this a hoax, too?"

"Did it sound like his voice?"

"I couldn't be sure. At first it did, but the connection was so bad. What reason would that woman in the flat have for telling me a lie, saying he was drowned if he wasn't?" Kate pressed her hands to her hot face. "Does everyone in this thing tell lies? What am I to believe? If that was Lucian speaking and not someone impersonating him, he says Francesca is in Somerset, near Taunton. But supposing I get there and find it's not true, that it's just another method of getting me out of the way."

"Poor Kate," said Johnnie, with rather helpless inconsequence. "As if anyone would want to get you out of the way."

"He said I was an interfering little fool. I don't think Lucian would have talked like that."

"Then it was a hoax, darling," Johnnie said soothingly. His eyes were both bewildered and admiring. "You're certainly a girl things happen to, aren't you? I've been here for days and everyone's mouth has been shut as tight as a clam's. You're here for five minutes and you get threatening phone calls."

"It's not funny!"

"No, darling, no. It's just that you're decorative enough to be conspicuous. When you arrive lights shine and bells ring. Look, drink your martini, and we'll do as we planned this evening. Have some dinner, and then drive out to see these people. If nothing comes of it, then we can mull over the situation. Anyway, who does this know-all think he is? You can't catch a plane at a minute's notice. You must sleep on it, at least, before you decide."

FIFTEEN

THEY MUST HAVE been some twenty miles out of Rome when the modest little Renault that Johnnie had hired broke down. It simply came to a quiet stop by the roadside, and Johnnie, after striking matches and vainly tinkering with the engine, had to admit that he knew almost nothing about cars mechanically, and that it looked as if they were stranded.

The situation was too old and hackneyed to be either amusing or particularly alarming.

Kate stood on the roadside, shivering a little in the cool wind that rustled the olive trees, and said coldly, "So what?"

"I say, dammit, I'm most awfully sorry. This will teach me to be more careful. I'm afraid the only thing to do is walk until we come to some kind of house or village. This is a little off the beaten track, unfortunately. We must be a good five miles still from the Torlinis. But I'm almost sure I remember a small *albergo* along this road somewhere. We can make for that. Or would you rather wait in the car?"

Kate looked around the empty countryside. The Italian moon, high and bright, showed the olive trees pitting the low slopes, the road a dusty white scar wandering into the darkness. There was no sound except the lonely rustling of the wind. It was an eerie and sombre landscape, like the mountains of the moon.

"I'm certainly not waiting in the car," she said tartly. "But you might have told me this was going to happen and I'd have worn walking shoes."

"You don't think I planned it!"

Johnnie's tone of outrage was so emphatic that it may have been assumed. But looking at the bulk of his figure, standing a little way off, perplexed and helpless, she couldn't even indulge in the stimulation of indignation.

"No, I don't suppose you did. It's too ridiculous a place to be stranded. Do you think we'll really find this *albergo*?"

"If we don't we'll come to the Torlinis. After five footsore miles. Dammit, what a bore this is. Come along, darling, I'll take your arm. It's terribly sweet of you not to be mad."

"I am mad," Kate said wearily. "But where does it get me?"

"Nowhere, my pet, I'm sorry to say. You're absolutely dead right."

Johnnie walked away with a swinging stride, surprisingly brisk for his slightly portly figure. At least the effort of keeping up with him had the advantage of shutting other things out of her mind. She stopped thinking of Gianetta's strange behaviour, and of the unexplainable telephone call she had had from someone who was presumably dead. Was Lucian really alive, she wondered, his fine austere features not smudged out of recognition by water and mud? She did not dare to dwell on the fact. There was nothing in her mind but the painful hardness and roughness of the dusty road beneath her high-heeled shoes, and the absurdity of being stranded in the Alban Hills, twenty miles from Rome. At least Johnnie was a cheerful person with whom to be stranded. William would have cursed and stormed and she would have had to calm him down. Then he would have burst out laughing and kissed her, and for a moment the infuriating situation would not exist. Suddenly she wanted very much to be at home in her basement flat, with William sprawling in the easy chair, scattering matches and tobacco about him, filling the air with pipe-smoke, and the deep lazy sound of his voice. It was the first time, she thought, that she had had this aching pull towards him. Almost as if, at this moment he also needed her. Curious. . . . Suddenly it was Johnnie tramping along, breathing noisily, beside her, Gianetta's lies, and the unidentifiable, distorted voice on the telephone that were myths. Francesca, too, was a myth. And this Italian moon lighting up the arid countryside. Scenes out of a film. Reality was back in her flat in London.

If only instead of being persuaded to pursue the mysterious Torlinis, she had stayed in the hotel to see if Lucian—or his impersonator—rang again. That, in the end, might have achieved better results. But she could no longer bear the static waiting. So here she was, ridiculously stumbling down the lonely road, stranded out of reach of telephones or news for goodness knew how long.

After a long interval, and a distance of perhaps two miles covered, there were suddenly lights around the bend in the road, an isolated twinkling of two windows and a swinging sign over a petrol pump.

"I was right!" Johnnie exclaimed in triumph. "It is the *albergo*. Jolly good show. You could do with a drink, I expect."

"And how," said Kate thankfully. Can you speak Italian?"

"Enough to make myself understood."

It was a shabby building, with a shutter flapping on an upstairs window, and the paint peeling beneath the lighted sign, *Albergo Garibaldi*. The half-open door led straight into a bar where a couple of men with flashing dark eyes and leathery skin leaned across the counter and an enormously fat barman refilled beer glasses.

Kate felt the three pairs of eyes fastened on her as Johnnie explained their predicament. It was as if they were summing her up, deciding whether she were a worthy cause for such a predicament. They would not for a moment think the breakdown of the car was genuine.

But it was genuine enough. Johnnie hadn't enjoyed the walk any more than she had. He was out of condition, and for the last half-mile had wheezed and made grunted exclamations of annoyance. He needed a drink more than she did.

He had a long and rather excited conversation with the barman, then brought two glasses of beer to the table where Kate sat and slumped down angrily.

"There's absolutely no one here who knows anything about cars. The best they can do is for Cesare—that scoundrel there"—he pointed to one of the lolling men—"to drive me into the next village and either find a mechanic or arrange for a tow."

"How long will that take?" Kate asked in dismay.

"Heaven knows. All night, probably. It's past eleven now, and these fellows have no idea of urgency. Tomorrow, next week, the next blasted year, will suit them. Frankly, darling, I think you'd better go to bed."

"To bed!"

"Our fat friend behind the bar who is, incidentally, the proprietor of this dump, says he has four bedrooms, all empty, all equally desirable. We may have two if we wish, though why we wish two—" Johnnie's eyes popped with a gleam of his old hearty humour. "Well, that's just another idiosyncrasy of the English. Actually, I don't expect I'll see much of mine, by the time I've collected that damn car."

There was no use in being angry. It was a quirk of fate that something, not tragic but farcical, happened each time she went out with Johnnie. The lights going out in the Paris night-club, and now this being stranded in a seedy-looking *albergo* with three frankly-puzzled inhabitants obviously discussing at length and with deep interest why two bedrooms should be required.

Kate shrugged fatalistically.

"Well, I can't sit here half the night being stared at. So I'd better have one of the rooms. But if you get back in reasonable time at all, we'll go back to Rome."

"Splendid," said Johnnie in a relieved voice. "I must say you're being a sport about this. No recriminations?"

"It could happen to anyone." Kate made the expected rejoinder mechanically. She already hated this place with its dreary brown walls, its dirty floor, the curled and shabby posters of impossibly blue lakes pinned on the walls. But perhaps the bedrooms would be better. Once again her mind was clouded with a mist of tiredness. She had suddenly to prop up her heavy eyelids with her fingers and remember who she was and why she was there.

Sitting in a dubious *albergo* in the Alban Hills was not going to find Francesca.

But did Francesca really exist at all?

A girl of seventeen or so, with a round, lively face, and wearing a rather grubby, peasant blouse that was cut much too low for the leering eyes in the bar, took her up an uncarpeted staircase to her room.

She unlocked the door with a flourish, displaying, with misplaced pride, what would have been better left undisplayed. Kate looked unenthusiastically at the iron bedstead, its brass knobs dull and fly-specked, the sunk-in-the-middle bed covered with a cotton spread, the cheap chest of drawers and mirror, also fly-specked, the unashamedly bare floor. There was dust on the window-sill and the chest of drawers. A mosquito whined in a thin ghostly sound, and periodically the hanging shutter outside flapped and creaked.

If Johnnie had really planned that breakdown he had done it with singularly little foresight. For even if he had meant, later, to burst through that thin door, who could imagine romance in a room like this?

Again the situation was farcical. But she was too tired to be amused.

The girl had a towel of doubtful whiteness over her arm. This she laid ceremoniously on the bed, and going to the open door pointed down the corridor. Kate realized she was politely indicating the toilet—there could not possibly be a bathroom in a place like this—and thanked her. The girl went out, closing the door.

Alone, Kate looked distastefully at the bed. She sat gingerly on its edge, feeling its unyielding hardness. Nothing, she thought, would induce her to get into it, or to undress. In any case, she had no night things. She would curl up on the cotton counterpane with her coat over her. If she were forced to spend the night here she must get a little sleep, for last night had been spent on the train, and once again, as so often in this turbulent fortnight, weariness was her enemy.

The mosquito continued to whine about the room. One could close the shutters, of course, but that would be unendurable. The cool wind that creaked the hanging shutter, and rustled in the olive trees, made the room chilly, though that was infinitely preferable to its inevitable stuffiness were the shutters closed. The only thing to do was to put out the light and lie down in the darkness and try to sleep a little.

She found her way to the distasteful toilet and had a sketchy wash. There did not seem to be anyone else on this floor. The four or five doors along the corridor remained closed, and no sounds came from within the rooms. Later, she supposed, Johnnie would come banging up to bed, but she hoped by then to be sound asleep.

When she put the light out the moonlight came in and softened the squalor of the room to the austerity of a cell in a monastery. Kate lay down and began to relax. The sounds outside were country sounds, a goat, tethered somewhere near, giving soft bleats, as if to its kid, the rustling of the olive trees, and someone's footsteps dying away down the road. The shutter creaked intermittently, and once there was a small outburst of voices from below, a woman's, shrill and rapid, and a deep, domineering man's voice, probably that of the stout proprietor. Then they ceased, but no footsteps came up the wooden stairs to bed. Obviously this, the guest floor, was untenanted except for herself, and later, Johnnie, if he did not wisely choose to doze in the car.

Creak, bang of the shutter, a cat on the prowl, lifting its thin lugubrious voice, the muttered baa-a of the nanny goat, the rustle of the olives, like a stiff, silk dress she had once had in which she had felt very sophisticated and gay and important. Her first dance dress. But the boy she had gone dancing with had not even particularly noticed it. He had been a youthful Johnnie, lapsing into silence, banishing the smooth romance that a moonlit night in the idyllic English countryside should have held. She had not, she thought, had the romance one dreamed of, the dark, exciting lover who spoke caressingly in her ear, and lifted her on to floating clouds. Lucian Cray might have done that, she thought drowsily.

But she had been stuck with the youthful Johnnie types, who talked about the Budget, and horses and the latest hunt, and then William, who was appallingly honest and left her no vanity, but who sometimes, unexpectedly, produced those floating clouds.

In spite of the hard bed, the whining mosquito, and the unfamiliar country sounds, she must have fallen asleep, for it seemed much later that she heard the fumbling at her door. Someone was opening it.

Not Johnnie! Oh, not Johnnie, she thought unbelievingly. That would be too ludicrous.

She sat up sharply and fumbled for the light. But the switch was at the door, of course. One could not expect a bedside switch in the *Albergo Garibaldi*.

"Who's that?" she demanded, as the opening door showed a deeper darkness beyond than the moonlight darkness of the room.

There was no answer, but the door closed, and a figure stood clearly within the room. A man's figure.

Kate pressed her hand to her mouth.

"Johnnie—if that's you—"

"It's not Johnnie," came a low, grating voice. "I've come to find out where you've hidden the diamonds. You'd better tell me quick."

The man was coming nearer. The moonlight caught his face for a moment, and Kate thought—surely she imagined—she recognized the Oriental cast of the features.

Oh, for a light! But the switch was beyond this menacing intruder, out of reach.

"Get out of here!" she whispered. "If you don't I'll scream."

"Where are the diamonds? That's all I want to know."

"I don't know what you're talking about," Kate gasped. She began to struggle off the bed, but suddenly her wrists were seized. The man's breath was on her cheeks. His face, dark, featureless, with only the faint, terrifying gleam of his eyes, was close to hers.

"If you don't want to end with Cray in the Tiber, tell me where you've hidden them."

"I don't know! I've never seen any diamonds! I don't know!"

Kate's voice rose. As she screamed the fingers tightened on her wrists. She struggled violently. The grip on her wrists was iron. For a moment she was held immobile.

"So you won't tell. We'll see about that. You wait."

Abruptly she was flung back on the bed and as quickly as a cat the figure moved across the floor, opened the door and was gone.

The door shut with a careful click. There was no need now for silence, for her scream must have aroused the whole house. In a moment someone—the round-cheeked girl, the fat proprietor—would come pounding up the stairs.

Kate lay breathing quickly, limp with shock.

Strangely enough, no one came. All at once the house was completely silent. As if there were no one in it at all except herself, and the violent intruder . . . who had melted away as quickly as a form in a nightmare. . . .

Kate struggled up and felt her way to the door to switch on the light. But the switch did not work. At least, nothing happened. She clicked it up and down uselessly and the light did not come on.

There must be a fuse, she told herself feebly. It couldn't be possible that her light was deliberately not functioning. Because it would not be advisable for her to look fully at her midnight visitor.

This was too much! She was leaving this room at once, and going downstairs to find someone. Where was Johnnie? Hadn't he come back? Why hadn't he heard her scream?

Angrily Kate fumbled for and found her shoes, and thrust her feet into them. She snatched up her bag and made for the door.

But the handle refused to turn. It was locked. From the outside.

For one minute, then, she gave way to panic.

She was locked in here to starve, to die. Unless she confessed the whereabouts of some completely mythical diamonds.

Was that why the Chinese-looking man had been stalking her—because he thought she was a jewel thief, or a diamond smuggler? But how had he crept into this hotel, and cared so little about her screams? Why was she locked in?

Kate flew to the window to look out hopefully. But the sill represented a sheer drop to the ground a long way beneath. She could not escape this way without a broken neck or, at best, a broken limb.

The mournful countryside, beneath the high, bright moon, showed no sign of life. There was only the ceaseless sound of the wind, and the creak of the banging shutter, a monotonous sound, as useless as her scream.

Kate looked at her watch and in the moonlight managed to see the time. It was half-past two.

Then where was Johnnie? He must be back by now. Had she slept so soundly she had not heard his return, and was he now sunk so deep in slumber that he did not hear her scream? She couldn't know. She could only sit rigidly on the side of the bed and think that in four hours or a little more it would be dawn, and then there must be someone walking by below whose attention she could attract.

But supposing the man with his cat's walk and his flat, yellow face came back, unlocking her door from the outside. . . .

It seemed to Kate that she could not turn her eyes from the dim shape of the door. But she had nodded and half-dozed before the careful turning of the key made her leap upright.

This time, as the door carefully opened, a sliver of light ran across the floor, then vanished as the door closed, and the intruder stood within.

"I warn you I'll scream the place down," Kate got out before, in her fright and the blurred darkness, she made out that this time her visitor was a woman.

"Oh, no, you won't, Kate, dear," came a friendly voice with the faintest Italian accent. A familiar voice. She had heard it before. Where?

"For one thing there's no one here to hear you. I mean, no one who will pay any attention."

"There's Johnnie!"

"Oh, him. He's not back yet. Cesare is seeing to him. But surely you remember me?"

An indolent voice from a couch, a pair of languorous dark eyes watching her, a petulant complaint that she was not strong enough to travel. . . .

"*Rosita!*" Kate exclaimed.

"None other." The woman crossed the room and sat on the bed beside Kate. She smelled of some expensive scent, her shape was curved and enticing. She was no longer an alien, deserted and peevish, in a foreign country. She was completely Italian, warm and low-voiced and conscious of her feminity.

"But how did you get here?" Kate demanded. "I've been looking for you. I wanted to tell you about Francesca. How on earth did you find me here, and where *is* Francesca?"

"I haven't a clue," Rosita answered languorously. "We really couldn't worry about her. Troublesome little creature."

"You mean you don't care about her!"

"Why should I? She's really no concern of mine."

"No concern! But she's your daughter!"

Rosita gave a light laugh. "That's what you think."

"She's not your daughter! That's a lie, too?" Kate peered exasperatedly into the darkness. "Why can't we have some light? What's wrong with this place? Why has someone locked the door? Why did that man creep in and ask me where the diamonds are? I know nothing about diamonds."

"Actually," said Rosita, in her soft, lazy voice, "that's what I want to know, too. Tell me what you did with them. You must have saved them when Francesca was kidnapped. Otherwise, why did you let her go? Come now, don't play the little innocent any longer. You're in this right up to your neck, and you know it. There'll be light, and the door will be unlocked when you've told us where you've hidden them."

Kate got up warily. She was measuring the distance from the bed to the door. But the other woman had suspected what she was doing, and quickly moved in front of her.

"Don't try that, Kate, dear. There's someone out there with a gun. We're quite serious, you know. We want those diamonds. They're valuable."

"For the last time," Kate declared angrily, "I know nothing about diamonds. If Francesca was carrying them—" She stopped as suddenly the thing began to come clear, the whole clever gamble that had so nearly come off. The doll, Pepita. The shabby doll with the hollow stomach. Pepita's diet was diamonds, cut or uncut, one didn't know which. But she was fed with them, and disgorged only for the little jet-eyed jeweller in Hatton Garden, Nicolas Grundy.

No wonder this succession of accidents and strange adventures had happened. There had been a continuous attempt to gain possession of the doll, and through her innocent, haphazard behaviour, sometimes carrying it with her, sometimes hiding it, she had unwittingly evaded the thieves.

But the thing had been a farce, anyway, for this time Pepita had not been carrying her hidden fortune, as no doubt she had done several times previously. Francesca must have discovered the hitherto unknown opening in her stomach, and thought it a clever place to hide a treasured but secret letter.

So she had started her journey with a valuable hoard, somewhere on the way she had lost it. And only Francesca knew where.

But this last information she must somehow keep from this woman who obviously cared nothing for a child's life. Because if she discovered, and Francesca's whereabouts were known . . .

Who in all the world was going to bother about a stray Italian child, lost and unclaimed. Who was going to report her disappearance to the police and stir up trouble?

"Yes?" said Rosita impatiently, "if Francesca were carrying the diamonds, what would she have done with them? Nothing, because she knew nothing about them. It was you who cleverly kept the doll. So come. You've given us enough trouble. We do not keep our patience forever."

"I have a loud voice," Kate told her. "In a moment I'm going to use it to call for help."

"Call away, call away," Rosita's voice was contemptuous. "I've told you no one will listen. Your precious Johnnie won't be back until morning if I know the sort of drinks he's been having. He's the party type, you know. He'll never make a successful detective."

With a sinking heart, Kate knew she spoke the truth. But this crafty Italian woman was not going to see her giving in.

"Bring in your bodyguard. Let him stand over me with a gun, if he likes. But you can't make me tell something I don't know. And I don't know anything about your filthy diamonds. Nothing. The doll had nothing but a letter written to a child inside it. And I, at least, don't lie. Now get out of here, and leave that door unlocked. If you have got away with one body in the Tiber, you're not going to easily get away with two. I'm here to find that poor, mistreated child, and I'm not going home until I find her. If you think you can frighten me, you're wrong."

"We'll see," murmured Rosita thoughtfully, "we'll see." Still keeping between Kate and the door, she suddenly made a swift movement and hastened out. The key was turned in the lock before Kate could spring after her.

The position was as it had been earlier, and there would be no help until Johnnie, stupid, greedy Johnnie, with a bad hangover, arrived in the morning.

Unless the man with the gun came in.

It was interesting, of course, to have so much explained. Now she knew why she had been constantly shadowed, why she had had those clumsy accidents. It had been supposed that either she was carrying the doll with its dangerous hidden hoard innocently, or else that she had carefully disposed of the contents of Pepita's stomach in a safe place. It had also been supposed that she may have been in league with Francesca's kidnapper.

For now it was certain the child had been kidnapped by someone perhaps even more unscrupulous than Rosita and her confederates. The awful thing now, if they believed her when she said she knew nothing about the diamonds, was that they would track Francesca down, like bloodhounds.

Somehow she had to find the child first.

Kate walked up and down the room, her footsteps echoing on the bare boards. The moon was sinking, its rays growing more golden and the room becoming darker. Now it was even too dark to see the time. Surely it must be morning soon and Johnnie would come back. Why didn't he come? How could he behave like this when he had known he was leaving her in a dubious-looking place.

But a knock-out drink would be nothing to the wicked Cesare. He would administer it with the greatest glee, and Johnnie, the gullible fool, would swallow it.

This organization must be powerful, for even in Paris, at that night-club, there had been the search made of her bag. And in London its octopus tentacles stretched.

She felt as if she hadn't slept for years. Her legs were crumpling beneath her. She was compelled to sit once more on the side of the bed, but she had a rigid determination not to fall asleep. Soon it would be morning. Nothing would seem quite so sinister by daylight. . . .

In spite of her efforts, she did doze, her head falling sideways against the hard iron bed-end. So that she didn't hear the door open the third time. It must have opened very softly, and her visitor entered like a ghost. For Kate's eyes flew open to see, in the gloom, a round, squat figure, with a very faint halo of white hair.

"Have a chocolate, Kate, dear," a cosy voice said.

Kate clapped her hands to her mouth. Now she could not speak at all. Mrs. Dix's voice! The little, round, too-plump figure with the white hair, the busy fingers fumbling in the chocolate box, the noisy sucking of a sweet.

But if the dead walked they did not eat!

"You won't have a chocolate? You young things, you worry too much about your figures. Now, Kate, dear, that little mission. You brought back the diamonds, didn't you? You mislaid the child, but that didn't matter because you had the diamonds. So where are they? Tell us and we promise you'll not be harmed."

"I—don't—know—"

"Come, dear, try to remember. The Tiber is very cold at this time of year, and muddy. Kittens are drowned in it. Not nice to swallow that water. So try to remember."

It was then that Kate's control broke. Anything real she could stand, but this ghost, this caricature, whatever it was, as uncanny as the face that had peered around the door in Mrs. Mossop's London house, was too much.

She began to scream. "You're not Mrs. Dix! Mrs. Dix is dead! You're only trying to frighten me! Go away! Go away, or I'll call the police!"

"The diamonds, dear? Remember?"

"I don't know anything about your horrible diamonds," Kate sobbed. "I wouldn't touch them if I were starving. I know nothing, I tell you. Nothing!"

Dimly she heard the cluck-clucking sound of remorse, then the cozy chuckle. She didn't realize she had her eyes tight shut, and only opened them at the sound of the door closing and finding herself once more alone.

Now she was trembling and dizzy. She lay back on the

uninviting pillow and the room swam in a sick swirl of stars and darkness. Then it faded away.

She must have become unconscious from fright and sheer exhaustion, for her half-faint melted into sleep, and when she opened her eyes with a dreadful start of nightmare awareness it was bright morning, and there was another tapping on her door.

"Tea, signorina," called a cheerful young voice, adding, "Please to enter, may I?"

But whoever it was couldn't enter, because the door was locked. Kate tried to speak, then didn't need to, for the door opened as if it were not even latched and the plump girl from the previous evening walked in with a tray and a beaming smile.

"*Buon giorno*, signorina." And then, obviously proud of her English, "Did you sleep well?"

"Sleep!" Kate echoed.

The girl's eyes flickered in surprise over Kate's rumpled but full-dressed appearance.

"You were too tired to take off your clothes, signorina?"

Kate sat up and looked at the breakfast tray. The china looked clean, the rolls were brown and appetizing, and the tea, though probably undrinkable, was a charming thought. They did these thoughtful things in Italy, she remembered—at least the Italy she had previously known. Faint energy and even reassurance stirred in her. If she were going to be murdered, at least it was going to be with the condemned criminal's due, a good breakfast.

"Thank you," she said, with automatic politeness. "Now there is something I want you to do, please. You understand me?"

"A little, signorina."

"Then tell the woman called Rosita I must see her at once."

"Rosita?" The girl frowned perplexedly. "I do not know anyone of that name."

"Now don't you go dumb on me, too. Rosita is here, staying in this God-forsaken *albergo*, and I want to see her at once."

'But I do not know. Honest! There is no woman here but

me." The girl smiled ingenuously, thrusting out her plump bosom.

"Then a little fat woman," Kate cried desperately. "Not Mrs. Dix, because Mrs. Dix is dead. I know she's dead. But someone who might have impersonated her."

"Please, signorina?"

"Someone who eats chocolates. *Cioccolata.*"

"You want *cioccolata*, signorina?"

Kate sighed and gave up.

"Is the signore back?" she asked wearily. "The signore with the car."

"*Si*, signorina. You did not hear? He made a great noise. But he has the headache. Oh, bad!" She giggled with naughty glee.

"One last thing," said Kate. "Switch on the light."

"The light? But it is day."

"I know it's day, but last night it wouldn't work. Or so I thought."

The girl gave a flip to the switch and the light sprang on, vying with the early morning sunshine. Her puzzled glance went back to Kate, whom by now she must have supposed to be quite crazy.

Perhaps she was crazy. Purely crazy, and not even simply the victim of a nightmare. Perhaps no one at all had come into her room during the night. There was nothing whatever to prove that they had. Only Johnnie's headache. But Johnnie may not have needed Cesare's potion to encourage him to linger in some bar where there was talk and laughter and liquor. Johnnie was unreliable. It seemed that it would be scarcely worth while even relating her nightmare, or whatever it had been, to him.

SIXTEEN

Johnnie was waiting in the bar which, by morning light, looked even more frowsty.

No one had watched Kate walk down the stairs. She had boldly opened the doors and looked into all the rooms on the top floor, and seen that they were indeed empty. This fact did not reassure her. Rather, it strengthened her unpleasant suspicion that the night may, after all, have been a long-continuing nightmare, and that if she were becoming a victim of such hallucinations she must be neurotic and it was time she went away for a long rest.

The yellow-faced man could well have been there, since he was her self-appointed shadow. But Rosita and especially Mrs. Dix—who lay in her narrow cold bed in a London suburban cemetery—must surely have been imaginary visitors. Even her screams, which so mysteriously went unheard, must have been the soundless ones of nightmare.

The plump maid was sweeping the passage that led into the kitchen. She smiled at Kate and waved her hand.

"*Arrivederci*, signorina," she called cheerfully.

Kate opened her bag and took out some of the squalid-looking lire notes. The girl thanked her profusely. She sang to herself as she returned to her sweeping. In a few years she would be fat and slatternly. But at present she was young and fresh and normal. There were no secrets in her merry, brown face. Kate was grateful for that, at least.

But Johnnie was another story. He was unshaven, bleary-eyed and full of apologies.

"I say, Kate, old girl, I really got into trouble last night. That Cesare! He's quite a lad. Did I get led up the garden path!"

"Is the car all right?" Kate asked briefly.

"Yes, good as gold. It was a faulty plug, the fellow said.

Cesare suggested a drink while we waited, and there it was. Fire water!" Johnnie shuddered. "God, I feel loathsome."

"Let's pay the bill and go," Kate suggested.

The stout proprietor behind the bar was watching them, a half smile on his face, his black eyes ironic. But he had looked like that last night. His face was no more secret or knowledgeable than it had been then.

Johnnie got to his feet.

"*Quanto debbo?*" he asked, and as the fat man laconically gave a figure he exclaimed, "My God, that for a night in this dump! By the way, Kate, you don't look any too brisk yourself. Did you get any sleep?"

"A little. When people weren't walking about. Ask him how many people live here."

Johnnie, occupied in sorting out crumpled lire notes, translated the question uninterestedly.

"He says only himself and his wife. The girl goes home at night."

The fat man went on talking, gesticulating and grinning.

"Oh, and a nanny goat and a kid and two or three cats. Business is bad at this time of the year. If you heard people walking about, angel, you must have been listening to ghosts."

"Yes," Kate murmured involuntarily. For one of them, at least, had been dead.

Voices and darkness . . . darkness and voices. . . . But the strange thing was that they had all had the recurring theme of diamonds. Whether it were intuition or reality, she was sure she had hit on the crux of the matter. Diamonds being smuggled into England by a child with a shabby, much-loved doll. That solution explained so much. And if it were so and it was found that the diamonds were no longer in the doll it really did mean Francesca was in danger.

But one would no longer confide in this sorry caricature of the spruce and self-confident Johnnie Lambert. He was not reliable and he couldn't see beyond his own nose.

"Let's go," she said urgently.

"Do we go straight back to Rome and forget the Torlinis?"

"Yes."

"Right. Wish I had an alka-seltzer. Confounded fool I've made of myself. Sorry and all that."

Kate was not concerned with his apologies. But she was alertly interested when, a little later, sunk in his remorse, Johnnie said defensively, "Actually I did make one discovery last night. That fat fellow at the *Albergo Garibaldi* knows the Torlinis. He said he'd never heard of them having a child. So it must be the wrong branch of the family. There are branches all over the place. He thought it would be the Florence one, but I checked that yesterday. The thing's a labyrinth. That's if there is a blasted kid. With all due respect to your evidence as an eye-witness, I strongly believe there isn't."

Later, as they became immersed in the stream of traffic pouring into the city, Johnnie turned to her. "What are you going to do now?"

"Have a hot bath when I get to the hotel."

"I mean after that."

"I haven't decided yet." She was going to see if there were any messages for her, any follow-up to the mysterious telephone call last night. She felt a strange certainty that there would be. But she no longer wanted to confide in Johnnie. It was extraordinary that Mrs. Dix should have employed him for a task needing diplomacy and finesse—unless she had deliberately chosen a bungler....

"Well, I'm throwing in my hand and going back to England. I've had this sort of thing. Needle in a haystack. If there is a needle at all. You'd better come with me."

"I don't think so."

She had to decide whether she would begin looking for that elusive needle in Somerset, as the voice on the telephone yesterday had told her to. But first there was the possibility of something having happened during her enforced night away. Her incurable optimism was showing itself again. She was not going to be defeated.

"I'll drop you at the hotel and go around to the airways

office," Johnnie said. "You'd better let me get a ticket for you."

"No, don't do that yet. I haven't made up my mind."

"Then make it up in that hot bath. I'll call you in an hour or so."

"That's very kind of you, Johnnie, but our excursions seem to be ill-fated. I think this is where we part."

"Honestly, Kate, I don't think you should stay here alone. You're too attractive, for one thing."

Kate laughed, avoiding his slightly bleary but anxious and sincere look.

"Johnnie, darling, if I fly with you we'll come limping into London Airport on one engine."

He scowled, not amused. "That's ridiculous nonsense. I'll still ring you later and see if you've changed your mind."

The clerk behind the desk at the Hôtel Romano gave her his welcoming smile, his dark eyes suggesting, with approval, that she was making the most of her time by staying out all night.

"You are enjoying Rome, signorina? You have had a wish at the Trevi fountain?"

"No, not yet."

"But you must throw a coin in the fountain, signorina."

And what would she wish for, Kate reflected. Francesca's safety, of course. Suddenly she felt helpless and frightened at the task ahead of her. With only Johnnie, stupid and drink-fuddled, to lean on.

"Tell me," she said casually, "are people often drowned in the Tiber?"

The young man, with his smooth, smiling face, looked startled.

"Sometimes, signorina. Regrettably. Too much *vino*, perhaps, or a wish not to live." He shrugged, abruptly changing from smiling welcome to melancholy.

"Has there been an Englishman drowned recently?"

"You mean yesterday, last week? No, not since the mystery of several weeks ago."

"Several weeks?"

"While the weather was still hot. It was said he had perhaps gone swimming in the moonlight, after a party, you know. It was all very suspicious, but the police could find out nothing more. He was dead, after all. Whatever the reason, he could not be brought back to life."

"What was his name?" Kate asked tensely. "Do you remember?"

"I do, because it was one of your strange English names." The young man gave his charming smile and enunciated carefully, "Gerald Dalrymple."

He looked at Kate anxiously and said, "That means nothing to you? He was not your friend?"

Kate was enormously relieved. "No, he was not my friend. That is the only drowning of an Englishman?"

"That is the only one I know of, signorina." The young man added with his impeccable manners, "I am sorry."

Kate picked up her room key. "Have there been any messages for me?"

"No. Nothing at all."

Now she didn't know what to think, but excitement was rising in her because, after all, that telephone call last night must have been from Lucian. He must be alive, thank heaven, and that also meant it must be true that Francesca was safely in Somerset. Now what should she do?

Nothing, she told herself, until she had had a long luxurious bath, and some food. After that she would be human again, and inspiration would come to her.

The inspiration did come to her while she was in her bath. She leapt out and only half-dry went to the telephone and asked for William's number in London. It was Saturday morning and he would not be at the office. She waited with an eagerness that caused her faint surprise, for the sound of his voice.

But when the call came through it was a woman's voice, vaguely familiar, that answered.

"Mr. Howard isn't here, I'm sorry."

"You mean he isn't in London?"

"No." The voice was cagey, and had that vague familiarity.

"Who is that speaking?" Kate demanded.

"Oh, Kate! That's Kate!" The far-off voice was raised in pleasure. "This is Miss Squires here. I'm staying in William's flat. But hasn't he told you?"

"How could he?" Kate returned, with some asperity. "I'm in Rome."

"But so is he, dear. He left by the early morning flight."

"Oh, the clot! Why can't he keep his nose out of my business? Then he should be here any time?"

"I believe they were held up by fog, but he should be on his way by now. I told him to go to the Hôtel Romano. Is that right?"

"So you're in this plot, too," Kate said disgustedly. "Well, I haven't time to talk about it now, but since William isn't there you'll have to do something for me. It's very urgent, and it may be a little difficult." She suddenly remembered Miss Squires sitting hunched and fearful in her cottage hugging her cat, and added doubtfully, "Will you try?"

"Of course," came the answer steadily. "I'm staying in William's flat. His housekeeper will look after Tom. What is it you want me to do?"

"There's a village somewhere near Taunton. I don't know its name, but I'm guessing it will be quite a small place. I think Francesca is there. She will be staying with a family called either Cray or Dalrymple. That's all I can tell you, except that they have two children called Tony and Caroline. If you can possibly find this family, will you tell them they *must* ask for police protection immediately. It's terribly important. I think they'll know what you're getting at."

Miss Squires' voice was not quite so steady now. "Are you sure Francesca isn't in Rome, then?"

"Not entirely. I want to stay a little longer to be sure. But this other thing is urgent. Do you think you can manage it?"

"I can have a jolly good try," Miss Squires' voice came back, with determined courage. "I know there's a lot more in this than I knew at first. But William will tell you. Goodbye, dear, and I'll ring you the moment I've got anything to report."

"Good girl," said Kate affectionately. "This all may be a hoax, so do be careful. Bless you."

So William was arriving at any moment. After a little while Kate's annoyance left her and she began to feel rather happy about it. Now she needn't feel even the faintest regret that Johnnie was deserting her. William was a much stronger leaning post. And a familiar one. If his car broke down, he would know how to fix it, at least. And also he possessed the incalculable asset of speaking Italian. He could do a little inquiring into the drowning of the mysterious Englishman, Gerald Dalrymple, which, Kate was now convinced, had been the beginning of the whole mysterious affair.

Now she was too excited to sit calmly waiting for William's arrival. On an impulse she scribbled a note:

> "Do I have no life of my own? Can't you leave me alone and attend to the roads of England, which are in much more immediate trouble than I am. I'm just dashing out to have another shot at getting Gianetta to talk. If you come while I am away don't move from this room!"

This she stuck in an envelope, addressed it to Mr. William Howard, and propped it on the dressing-table. She would ask the desk clerk to give William her key. He would not quibble at that. He would smile approvingly, and ask her again if she were enjoying Rome, and had she thrown a coin in the Trevi fountain. And there would be no shadow of drowned men or little girls in deadly danger in his bright, friendly eyes.

Just before she left, the telephone rang again. She snatched it up eagerly, hoping that it would be Lucian Cray, with a better connection this time so that she could hear what he said.

But it was Johnnie. She felt rather flat. Poor Johnnie. And he meant so well.

"Hi, Kate. Changed your mind about coming with me?"

"No. William's arriving."

"Who's William?" His voice sounded suddenly peevish and suspicious.

"Oh, just an old friend of mine. He has rather a thing about keeping an eye on me." She knew she was being smug, but the memory of Johnnie's bleary-eyed ineffectiveness rankled.

Johnnie gave a sudden snort of laughter. "So you look for the lost brat and your boy-friend looks for you, and who looks for him? This is becoming a farce."

"Yes, isn't it," said Kate pleasantly. "William knows about cars, too. So you can leave me quite safely."

There was a short silence. "Suppose I deserved that." His voice was lugubrious, and Kate was suddenly ashamed of herself. "But I still think you should come with me. I'll take a wager you don't get any further ahead than I did with your search, William or no William. Or have you had any more mysterious phone calls?"

"No."

"Too bad. You're quite sure you didn't hear the name of that place in Somerset?"

"No, I didn't. I wish I had."

"H-m-m. Well, I've got a booking on the afternoon flight. I rather think I'll take it, you know."

"Don't wait for me," said Kate coolly. "Good luck, Johnnie, and goodbye."

"I think you're being rather reckless, my dear."

"Why? Are you afraid I'll fall in the Tiber, too?"

Johnnie gave his loud, hearty laugh. "Not at all. You're a clever girl. You're too good at taking care of yourself."

Taxis to the street off the via Appia were becoming a luxury. Kate ambitiously took a tram, edging her way into its crowded interior, and clinging hard to a strap as it rocked and clattered down the busy streets. She was alternately flung against garlic-redolent working men who ogled her, and old women in their inevitable black, gnawing at hunks of bread and staring at her with slightly resentful eyes. She wanted badly to sketch their brown, withered faces, their hooded eyes that had tantalized Michelangelo and Leonardo da Vinci centuries ago. The sun shone; the chestnuts and acacias reluctantly relinquished their foliage, deliberate leaf by leaf; the tram rattled on, and the city was vibrant with noise and movement.

But the narrow, shabby house in the little street was completely silent. No one came in response to Kate's knock. She waited a little, imagining that Gianetta's dark eyes, like those of a timid captive animal, were peering secretly at her through the window. If they were, Gianetta obviously was not going to open the door.

Kate stepped back, feeling baffled and frustrated, and also conscious of growing apprehension. Those silent, dark rooms of the house could be hiding anything, anything. . . .

She noticed that two or three women in the street had gathered to watch her. She walked towards them, asking optimistically, "*Parla Inglese?*"

Their heads shook regretfully. Then one of them raised her voice and with the shrill Italian intonation called, "Maddalc-cc-na !"

A door opened and a young girl of about sixteen came out. The woman who was apparently her mother pointed at her and explained, "She speak *Inglese*, signorina."

The girl gave a shy smile, and Kate said, "I came out here to see Gianetta, but there doesn't seem to be anyone home. Do you know where she is?"

"She has gone to England. Last night late she left."

"To England !" But that couldn't be true. Not shabby little Gianetta, who had obviously never ventured more than a few miles from her home in all her life.

"*Si*, signorina. To see her daughter who is sick. She had to go quite quickly. And this morning the man came to do the floor but he couldn't get in."

"Did he get in?" Kate asked tensely.

"Through the window." The girl giggled. "Some boards were quite decayed, he said. There is a lot of work to do. Poor Gianetta. She has many troubles."

"Did you know she had a daughter in England?" Kate asked.

"Oh, yes. Francesca. We have always known Francesca." The girl shrugged. "But she has a wealthy grandmother in England—I think Gianetta once worked in her house—and she makes many visits."

"You speak English very well," Kate said automatically.

"Oh, yes. I go to classes."

The circle of watching women, with their avid, baffled eyes, was disturbing, like being watched by a jury of crows who would pronounce some unintelligible verdict. Kate could not take in the information that Francesca was Gianetta's child. No wonder she had looked so aged, so frightened, now that something had gone seriously wrong with those mysterious journeys to England. No wonder she had been so scared and secretive yesterday. How did she know who she could trust?

"The man who came to do the floor," she asked. "What did he look like?"

The girl paused a moment. She said something in rapid Italian to the other women, and they began to nod, their eyes sparkling with amusement.

"We all say," she told Kate, "that he must have come a long way to get to Rome. Or else his mother had." She giggled again, enjoying her cleverness. "We thought he was Chinese."

Kate did not enjoy her journey back by tram In spite of its rattling bustle, it was much, much too slow. She could not get back quickly enough to see if William had arrived and to tell him of this latest development. For she was so afraid, so dreadfully afraid, that Gianetta had not gone to England, that on the contrary she had not gone far at all. But also that it was unlikely she would ever come back....

The clerk greeted her with his unfailing smile, and an air of delight. "Your friend has arrived, signorina."

"Oh, thank heaven! Is he waiting?"

"I gave him your room key as you advised."

"Thank you. I must see him quickly."

She ran up the stairs, not waiting for the lift, and burst

into her room. "William, you crazy—" she began, but stopped as the man rose from the chair at the window.

He was not William.

"Sorry to disappoint you, Kate," said Lucian Cray.

SEVENTEEN

THERE WAS NO time to exchange polite greetings. Kate burst out, "They've got Gianetta. What are we to do?"

At least his face did not go blank. He did not say, "Who is Gianetta?" and pretend ignorance, as she had grown accustomed to expect. He said quietly:

"Don't worry. She's halfway to England by now."

"You don't believe that story!"

Although his voice was quiet, his eyes were narrowed and hard. His face still excited her—or perhaps it was the artist in her whom it excited—but now she saw its ruthlessness, and its dedication to some unwavering purpose. He would not be an easy person to live with, or an easy enemy to have.

"Why didn't you go when I told you to?" he repeated.

She flung up her head. "How could I be sure you were telling me the truth?"

"No, I suppose you couldn't be sure, after all that has happened." He regarded her thoughtfully.

"How did you know I was here, even?"

"I have methods as well as Johnnie Lambert."

Kate started a little at that, but the unreality of it all was too much for her.

"I came here thinking you were drowned!"

"Who told you that?"

"Oh, some woman in the upstairs flat of your house in St. John's Wood. It was your house, I suppose?"

"Yes, my house. But not my body in the Tiber." The hard ruthlessness had come back into his face.

"No, the clerk downstairs told me whose that was. Gerald Dalrymple's. But who was he?"

"He was my sister's husband," Lucian said sombrely.

"Oh, how dreadful! Tony's and Caroline's father! The person who wrote the letter to Francesca."

"Exactly. You found out too much, Kate. Even I didn't know about that letter."

"But you knew about the diamonds," Kate said breathlessly.

His eyes pierced her. "How did you find out about them?"

"I had a nightmare last night that people were accusing me of having them. Me! And when I woke up I knew somehow that I had dreamed the truth."

"Didn't I tell you last night to go home, that it wasn't safe."

Kate's eyes widened. "Then it wasn't a nightmare? Were those people really there, in my room in the dark? Even Mrs. Dix—" Her mouth was dry.

"My God, not Mrs. Dix!" he exclaimed. "Whose picturesque flight of imagination was that? Poor Kate! Was it very bad?"

"I screamed my head off. But no one seemed to hear. The wretched place might have been completely empty. That was why it was so fantastic and horrible—so that by daylight I was sure I had been dreaming. I didn't even tell Johnnie. He was too stupid, anyway, and I wasn't sure then that I trusted him."

Lucian gave a tight smile. "Did you tell Johnnie where Francesca was?"

"I told him I'd had your telephone call that she was in Somerset. After all, that was only fair since we were both looking for her. But we thought we'd look up this branch of the Torlini family first. Then the car broke down. . . ." Her voice died away. She said, very slowly, "Shouldn't I have told Johnnie?"

"It's exactly what I hoped you would do. You couldn't have done better—beyond, of course, keeping your inquisitive nose out of the whole business."

Kate felt for a chair and sat down. "What are you trying to tell me?"

"If you hadn't had a kind heart, Kate, I'd have been no further ahead at all, and my poor sister might never have discovered the truth about her husband's death. But thanks to your impulsiveness and your friendliness and your utterly enchanting feminine tendency never to stop and think, we're getting somewhere. Now you say Johnnie has left for Somerset."

Kate nodded miserably. "He was catching the afternoon plane. But he didn't know where in Somerset to go. I couldn't hear what you were saying on the telephone."

"I didn't mean you to. London Airport will be enough. What's wrong, Kate?"

Kate pressed her fingers to her eyes. She couldn't bear that he should see her tears. In his dry, summing-up voice he would make more remarks about her feminine warm-hearted qualities. And she didn't want to be analysed by Lucian Cray. She wanted William to roar at her, "Kate, you clot, I've a good mind to beat you."

"Shouldn't William be here by now?" she asked tightly.

"That's who you were expecting?"

"Yes. I just heard he'd followed me, to look after me, or something. He does utterly mad and unnecessary things like that."

"I wouldn't say it was unnecessary or particularly mad," Lucian remarked "If you were my fiancée I'd keep you on a leash."

"I'm not William's fiancée," Kate snapped, with taut nerves.

"No?" Lucian eyed her reflectively. "I still wouldn't trust you out of my sight. One day you'll stick that pretty neck out too far."

"It's nothing to do with you what I do with my neck."

"No, it isn't, after all. What I think you need is some food."

"I'm not hungry." She had controlled her brief weakness, and said more calmly, "Tell me the rest of this fascinating story. Francesca's doll was filled with diamonds, which she discovered, thought they were a lot of dirty stones, threw them away, and put what she valued much more, a letter from your brother-in-law, in their place. He had been coming to Rome and secretly making friends with her, is that right?"

Lucian nodded. "Go on, Kate."

"So now that I was put through the third degree last night, and it was more or less proved that I hadn't got the diamonds, and am up to my neck in this affair only because I'm crazy enough to care what happens to a stray child, someone has been tearing up the floorboards in Gianetta's house, and someone else is dashing off to find Francesca and frighten her out of her wits until she tells where she put those dirty old stones. Or indeed how she found that her doll split in half. I imagine the opening was pretty well concealed until she did it up clumsily again."

"Kate, your acumen is fairly bright, after all. That's what I assume has happened."

"Were the diamonds cut or uncut?" she asked inconsequentially.

"I'm not sure. There was a jewel robbery in Venice not long ago when a Contessa lost her diamond necklace. It was valued at thirty thousand pounds. I may be wrong, but I think that's what we're looking for. It would be broken up, of course."

"And that's what I've been carrying about in that snake-doll, Pepita!" Kate exclaimed in horror.

"What everyone thought you were carrying about."

Involuntarily Kate began to chuckle with wry amusement. "Mrs. Dix and Nicolas Grundy and my shadow, the Chinese gentleman, who fortunately is always just one step too many behind, and Mrs. Mossop."

"Mrs. Mossop is Mr. Grundy's sister," said Lucian, "and, incidentally, usually wears a wig. But perhaps deliberately leaves it off at times. I believe you got a fright there one day."

"Then it was she who looked into the room, It was a head like an egg, featureless, utterly horrible." Kate shivered as it all came to her. "I was supposed to be asleep from drugged sherry, and naughty Pepita, full of diamonds, was unguarded in my bag. But I ran away!" she said disgustedly.

"It wasn't from courage but from warm-heartedness that you got into this," Lucian reminded her.

"Yes, I suppose so. And what about that old woman in Rosita's room, and the way the room had *aged*?"

"Easy enough to do. An old woman can soon scatter a sort of cobwebbing of her bits and pieces about a room. You were awkward about wanting to see Rosita, so some place had to be arranged for her. I'm not sure, but I think that old woman is another sister of Mr. Grundy."

"Is Mr. Grundy the big noise behind all this?"

"No," said Lucian slowly, "not completely."

"How do you know all these things?"

"Oh—I have my shadows, too. My brother-in-law Gerald was in this game professionally. He'd taught me a few things about private detection."

"Better than my efforts," Kate said regretfully.

"On the contrary. I'm sorry to say that you've been my decoy. It wasn't meant to be this way. It was your own behaviour that started it."

But he *had* let her walk into danger, Kate thought. He was brilliant and fascinatingly attractive, but that steel-hardness in him that allowed him to use a child and a woman to achieve his ends left her feeling cold and a little repelled.

"There's a gang of international thieves and smugglers at work," he went on. "Gerald had been employed by one of the big insurance companies to try to get on to their racket. He'd found out something big, but unfortunately didn't live to tell it. Francesca was one of his clues. He'd made friends with her and talked about his own children, Tony and Caroline. When he died Gianetta was too scared to talk. She's a widow and had been a maid in the house of one of these people. She was bribed and terrified into letting Francesca be one of the children to have an occasional trip to England. She hated it, but what could one poor woman with a child to support do against that sort of pressure. When Gerald died the thing became a nightmare to her. She somehow got hold of his diary, and took a big risk in sending it to my sister. There was just enough information in it for me to start on."

"So you kidnapped Francesca!" Kate exclaimed indignantly.

"Merely borrowed her, Kate, dear. I arranged for a friend to meet the train at Basle, and we'd whisk her off. All those schoolchildren were a godsend. They prevented, as you know, your giving the alarm until morning."

He met her outraged gaze.

"I'm sorry, Kate. I didn't know you then. I thought you'd go home and forget about it, especially when I was pretty certain there wouldn't be a public fuss made. But you began to be quite a trouble—"

"You callously kidnap a child—" Kate began.

"Not callously. Francesca was very happy about going to see Tony and Caroline at last. I talked to her for a moment in the train when you were out of the compartment, and she was very excited. You noticed that yourself. She's quite a girl, by the way. She's been kept as much as possible from learning English, in spite of her trips, and she's also been trained not to talk."

"Heading for the secret service, no doubt," Kate said dryly.

Lucian ignored her interruption, and went on, "My friend Peter brought her by car from Basle to Paris, and she even had her ascent of the Eiffel Tower."

"So it *was* her I heard!"

"Kate, believe me, I didn't mean to get you into all this trouble. I thought Francesca would have the diamonds on her, stitched in her clothes, or something. The wretched doll never occurred to me. But she hadn't got them so there was I, with a stolen child, whom no one was at all interested in because they knew she hadn't got the loot. My bait had completely failed, and I had inadvertently got you into danger. You had the doll, after all, and everyone thought it was full of diamonds. Except you and me. And Francesca, of course."

Kate gave a wan smile.

"Thanks to my stupidity, I never realized I was in real

danger. Even in Paris, when the lights went out in that fishy night-club, I thought it was all accidental." That brought her thoughts back to Johnnie Lambert, and she said slowly, "Lucian—which side is Johnnie on? Why are you so glad he's left for England?"

His eyes were enigmatic.

"My bait's been swallowed at last. Extradition orders aren't easy to get without pretty good evidence. They can hold him there on a false passport charge, to begin with."

"But he's so stupid! Surely he's not the big fish."

Lucian looked at her with his narrowed, hard eyes.

"The big fish, Kate, dear, is Major Dix."

"Mrs. Dix's dead husband!"

"Mrs. Dix's very-much-alive husband." Lucian didn't give her time to dwell on that startling information. "Now we've got two things to do. Find where Francesca put the diamonds—Gianetta swears she knows nothing—and see when your friend William is due in. I suggest ringing the airport first."

"And then do we go back to England to question Francesca?"

"I've questioned her until I'm blue in the face. She's a child of few words. She just goes blank and says she doesn't understand. She's the original Mona Lisa."

Kate smiled reminiscently.

"She's a remarkable child. Is she really safe now?"

"She's never been in danger, as far as she knows. She's having a whale of a time, refusing to speak English and demanding enormous platefuls of ravioli. But you'll see for yourself soon enough."

"I can't believe it. What utter heaven! Who cares about the loathsome diamonds?"

EIGHTEEN

AT FIRST LUCIAN could get no satisfaction from the airport.

"They say the last flight from London Airport came in two hours ago."

"But that must be the flight William was on. Miss Squires said he had left ages ago. Why isn't he here?"

"Don't panic," said Lucian. "They're going to check and call me back. Let's see if we can get some sandwiches and coffee sent up."

"You can eat," Kate said, clenching her hands and beginning to walk about the room trying to combat her now familiar apprehension.

"And so can you." Lucian's cool eyes surveyed her. "Look at you. Thin and haggard. Is that any way to greet your fiancé?"

"I told you he isn't my fiancé. We're not even good friends. Or amicable friends." Kate's voice was curt with nervousness and suspense. "But if that plane came in two hours ago why isn't he here? He's an editor and a writer. He's not used to this sort of thing. He's done something foolish—"

"If it comes to that, you're both babes in arms," Lucian said with his air of detached amusement. "It's a good thing you're an attractive young woman."

"Why?" Kate asked, with her sharp suspicion.

"Italians—and other nationalities—are rather susceptible to pretty girls."

Was that why she had been allowed to come back safely after last night? She remembered Johnnie, with his sudden wistfulness, saying, "It's a pity you're so attractive."

"William isn't a pretty girl," she said involuntarily. "He hasn't that invisible weapon, or whatever it is."

"He's probably looking at the Pantheon. Relax, Kate.

Didn't we say on the train that it will be the same in a thousand years."

Kate made an impatient exclamation. "You can't apply that theory to moments of tension! They last for ever."

The telephone rang. Kate jumped nervously.

Lucian spoke into it in Italian. Was it her imagination that his face tightened? He abruptly turned his back to her. The quick, unintelligible words flowed on maddeningly.

Then he put down the receiver and turned.

"What did they say? Where's William? Hasn't he come?"

"Yes, he came by the last flight, a couple of hours ago. But he didn't travel into the terminal by the airways bus. He seemed to meet friends, and they left by car."

"Friends!" Kate exclaimed. "Who would he know? Unless it was someone he travelled with who gave him a lift. But in that case why isn't he here by now?"

"They've stopped for drinks, perhaps. I wonder what's happened to those sandwiches. I'll go down and shake someone up."

"Lucian, don't be absurd! William wouldn't stop two hours for drinks, not when his whole object in coming here was to find me. He is absentminded, I know, but when he's doing a thing, he goes straight to it. He hasn't stopped for drinks. What's happened to him? Oh, God, this awful nightmare again!"

Lucian took her hands and held them a moment, firmly.

"It'll be all right, Kate. Believe me! He's probably forgotten the name of the hotel. Now just wait here while I run down and see a friend of mine. And I'll be back with the sandwiches in a moment."

It was while he was gone that the telephone rang again. Kate stared at it a moment, hynotized. Then suddenly she snatched it eagerly, expecting William's voice.

"Is that Miss Tempest speaking?" came a clipped, English voice.

"Yes, who is that?" English, she thought, in relief. The people who gave William a lift in from the airport.

"It isn't of importance to you who is speaking, Miss Tempest. But just for the record, it's Major Dix. We have your friend, Howard, with us. Rather against his wishes, I'm afraid. But as soon as we locate what all of us are looking for we'll let him go."

"The diamonds!" Kate gasped.

"Exactly."

"But you know I haven't the slightest clue where they are!"

"Oh, come now, you don't mean to tell me that your friend Cray hasn't got the child to talk. If he hasn't he's a damn fool, and I'm giving you three hours to do so. That's ample time to do a little telephoning to Somerset. I'll call you again at six o'clock. After that it will be dark."

"What do you mean?" Kate whispered.

"More than one foreigner has stumbled drunk into the Tiber." The clipped, cultured voice became contemptuous. "You amateurs shouldn't take on these jobs. They always have fatal results."

"You can't do this!" Anger and fear made Kate raise her voice vehemently. "William is perfectly innocent."

"Then let him stick to his pen."

"We'll call the police—"

"A search would take a long time. Much longer than the time of the moon's rising. Let's be poetic about it, shall we? There's my proposition. The diamonds for your friend's life. Fair enough?"

The telephone clicked just as Lucian came back into the room, followed by a waiter with a tray of coffee and sandwiches.

"Kate! What's happened?"

She had to wait until the waiter had put down the tray and gone out. The disastrous unfairness of this happening to William, who was perfectly innocent, made her forget to be afraid. She was filled with anger and indignation.

She heatedly told Lucian what had happened, and added, "I know where he'll be. At the *Albergo Garibaldi*. I'm sure that's their headquarters. We've got to go at once. Have you got a car?"

Lucian's hand was on her shoulder. "Sit down and tell me again calmly what has happened and exactly what this man said. Here! Have a mouthful of this."

He produced a flask from his pocket and unstoppered it. The neat brandy made Kate gasp, but it steadied her panic.

She related the telephone conversation again, and saw, in a detached way, Lucian's eyes gleam and his mouth tense with excitement.

"The big fish," he said softly, "we've almost hooked him."

"Almost hooked him when you don't even know where he is. And we have this ghastly time limit."

Lucian picked up the telephone and spoke for a moment. Then he put a sandwich into Kate's hand and poured coffee.

"Giovanni's bringing around the car. He'll be a few minutes. He's a fast driver. Are you nervous?"

"Not any longer of simple things like fast cars," Kate said wryly.

"Yes, it's all a matter of proportion, isn't it? Do you want to tidy up before we leave? I'll wait for you downstairs. I'm not at all sure that this *albergo*, fishy though it sounds, is the place to go. They'll surely know that you remember it all too well. But I'd like to have a look at it."

"Not only the *Albergo Garibaldi*, but the Torlinis' villa farther on. That could be the place."

When Kate was alone she washed her face and combed her hair, and swallowed some more coffee. She couldn't eat. Then she looked around the room with a feeling of surprise that it could seem so ordinary and innocent. One had always heard that drama took place in hotel bedrooms, but one had never expected it to happen to oneself. Not even in Rome, with the forgotten centuries hanging in stone over the noisy, hurrying, effervescent people. Later, she told herself, she and William together would throw coins in the Trevi fountain, and wander in the silence and peace of the Colosseum, where autumn had beheaded the wild flowers growing in the stone cracks, and taken the scent from the vanilla trees.

Let Johnnie Lambert be arrested at London Airport for his false passport. (How had Lucian cleverly discovered that he travelled with a false passport?) Let Gianetta be reunited with her silent, stubborn daughter, and Miss Squires go back safely to her cottage and her cat. Let justice be done over the grave of a drowned Englishman.

But she and William would have their snatched hours of happiness in Rome. How utterly blind and foolish of her never to have realized that William would be the perfect travelling companion. Even if he had two black eyes and a multiplicity of bruises. For he would not have been overpowered easily, and he had a violent temper when aroused.

Oh, William, William, please let me be allowed to look after your black eyes. . . .

Giovanni, a slim, smart, flashing-eyed young man, drove extremely well. Although he doubled on his tracks now and again to throw off any pursuer, Lucian explained, he seemed to know the way through the autumn-melancholy countryside to the *Albergo Garibaldi*. When Kate commented on this fact, Lucian said, "Oh, he's been there before." And added cryptically, "We were looking after you as well as possible last night. You are too unpredictable to look after with complete certainty."

Giovanni gave her his flashing smile, the inevitable admiration in his eyes. Kate expected him, too, to ask if she had had a wish at the Trevi fountain, and she wondered absurdly whether he had disguised himself as the goat or the prowling cat last night. Nothing was real to her any more. It was years ago that she had seen a stout little girl in a white starched dress setting out hopefully on a journey.

A deadly little girl who had indirectly robbed Mrs. Dix of her life, Kate of her dearest friend, and Pepita of her stomachful of treasure.

It was siesta time at the *Albergo Garibaldi*. By daylight it looked even more squalid, with the faded paint peeling off the shutters, and a piece of fallen plaster disclosing the bare ribs of the wall within. Giovanni waited in the car. Lucian told Kate to come with him, and together they rang the jangling bell for some time before the stout proprietor, sleepy-eyed and unshaven and reeking of garlic, appeared.

The merest flicker of alarm passed over his face. Then he bowed and leered with repulsive friendliness.

"Ah, so the signorina returns."

"She finds your place irresistible," Lucian said ironically.

Kate's mouth opened in surprise. "You couldn't speak English last night!" she accused.

The man grinned impertinently. "The signorina did not inquire. What can I do for you? I regret we are closed at this time of day."

"We just want to have a look over your place."

"Sorry, signor. We are closed. Later, with pleasure."

"That's too late," Kate cried impetuously. Lucian's fingers tightened warningly on her arm.

"Oh, too bad, too bad," said the man in his oily manner. "But the country is more attractive by moonlight." His black, bold eyes rested significantly on Kate. Their look did not suggest anticipated amours, but the danger that could come by night with the rising of the moon.

Lucian beckoned to Giovanni, who slid out of the car and came over.

"We will look over your place now, signor. My friend has a search warrant. Come along, Kate. Show us the room where you had your visitors last night." He turned to say sardonically to the startled proprietor, "You should hire a theatre if you enjoy amateur theatricals."

The leer was replaced by a ferocious frown. The fat man slowly stepped back to let them into the squalid bar.

"Whatever your business," he said, in a voice suddenly shrill, "you will find nothing here."

Nor did they. Swiftly, because of time running out, they went over the shabby, bare-floored bedrooms upstairs, and downstairs the large, dark kitchen in which the round-faced maid stared at them speechlessly, shaking her head violently to all Lucian's brief questions, the backyard, where the goat and kid were tethered and a few scrawny hens pecked in the dust, and the two rooms at the back which were obviously the living quarters of the proprietor and his wife.

The woman, as stout as her husband, garbed in black, and

scowling with suspicion, sat in the stuffy living-room, and refused to speak. Her plump hands were folded stubbornly in her capacious lap. Her lips were clamped together. She remained immovable while they took a quick look in the bedroom beyond. She was a frowning Buddha scattering unspoken curses on them.

"Nothing here," said Lucian. "Let's go."

But there was. Kate picked up a half-empty box of chocolates from the sideboard and passed it to the woman.

"Have a chocolate, dear," she said in a cooing voice.

The woman's head jerked back. Her eyes widened. Slowly she shook her head. But now it wasn't that she wouldn't speak, she couldn't. Her fear was too obvious.

In the car Lucian slipped his arm along the back of the seat around Kate's shoulders.

"Well done," he said. "First clue. I'll bet that dear, kind soul speaks English without an accent. She looks like a retired variety artist. It's a pity we haven't time at present to check. To the Torlinis', Giovanni, and step on it."

"What's the time?" Kate asked nervously.

"Four-fifteen. We're doing fine."

"Lucian, do you think Mrs. Dix was murdered?"

"I haven't a doubt about it. By her loving husband. But for precisely what reason, I'm not sure. Look, there's the villa. On the hillside among the cypresses. Nice place it looks, as the country residence of a crook."

It looked like the summer residence of a millionaire. There was an orderly row of cypresses leading up to a wide terrace. Slim white ladies, cast in stone, were grouped around the central fountain and made a pale glimmer in the cypress groves. The house itself was of pink marble.

Kate suddenly felt extraordinarily scruffy and jaded. Lucian gave her a sardonic look as she hastily smoothed her hair.

"Don't worry about that. You're not meeting a Prince of the Borghese or even of the Medicis. You're meeting—I hope —a thief and a murderer."

Giovanni said something in his own language to Lucian, and Lucian gave a short, ironic laugh.

"Giovanni says why didn't we discover this place for ourselves, why was it left to you, a girl, to do it."

"We don't even know whose place it is."

"We'll soon find out," Lucian said confidently.

This was not so easy, however. A very old servant opened the door. He looked half blind but he had a wrinkled, crafty face which Kate suspected did not miss much. He talked for a little in a high, quavering voice, shrugging his shoulders and waving his hands. Lucian turned to Kate.

"He says the family are all away. They've gone to spend the winter in Naples. I think we'll take a look, all the same. Keep those sharp eyes of yours open, Kate."

Another inhospitable doorstep, thought Kate. She looked at her watch and her panic grew. Time was running out. Already the daylight was fading. Surely William was not concealed in this large, luxurious house. If he were, he would be making a great noise.

"Make it fast," Lucian said to Giovanni. "We can pick up less important evidence another time."

The old man seemed bewildered, but he understood what Giovanni's badge meant. He hastily stood back, mumbling to himself, as they went in. He did not attempt to follow them, for there seemed nothing to hide. The large reception rooms were dust-sheet shrouded, and upstairs the airy bedrooms, with their fine views of the cypresses and the olive groves, were the same.

At another time Kate would have wanted to linger, looking at the pictures, the statuary and the personal relics of the absent family. As it was, in her despair that this great sleeping house would produce any clue as to William's whereabouts, she noticed only one significant thing. That was a photograph of a young woman with large, dark, hooded eyes, and a petulant mouth. She was dressed in the style of ten years earlier. It took a second glance for Kate to realize it was Rosita, the woman who had lain languidly on the couch in London and posed as Francesca's mother.

So Rosita's natural habitat was not the squalid *Albergo*

Garibaldi. It was this expensive villa, with its marble floors and the constant sound of fountains playing.

This information seemed to give both Lucian and Giovanni satisfaction. Their quarry, though absent at present, was being run to earth. But would it be unearthed before the rising of the moon?

"Lucian, William isn't here. I know he isn't. The place feels empty. We're wasting our time."

In which of these lofty rooms had Johnnie Lambert sat drinking with Cesare and the half-blind caretaker while keeping out of the way of the amateur theatricals that were taking place at the *Albergo Garibaldi*?

It didn't matter. They had to get another inspiration quickly.

Giovanni said something and Lucian nodded. "There's money in this racket, all right. Giovanni says that group looks like a Bernini."

"Oh, for heaven's sake, we're not on an art appreciation tour!" Kate exclaimed. "I think we've made a mistake. We should have stayed in Rome. Let's go back. After all, the Tiber—"

"Bodies can be transported by car," Lucian said, with unthinking callousness. "Giovanni is going to take a quick look in the cellars. But I think you're right, Kate." Then he patted her shoulder. "Cheer up. This trip hasn't been wasted. We've discovered Mrs. Dix's ghost, and we know Rosita lives here. Probably her family previously owned this place, but it takes illicit wealth to keep it up now. My guess is that she's Major Dix's mistress."

"And Mrs. Dix found out, just the other day!" Kate said intuitively. "That would be it. She adored her husband, you know. She pretended to revere his memory, but really it was his live self. She probably agreed to do anything for him, no matter if it were illegal. And then she must have found out suddenly that he was making love to Rosita. It would shake her badly. Perhaps she threatened to go to the police."

"I think you've got it, Kate. This character has his deserts coming to him. But long overdue. Here's Giovanni. Now, Kate, shut your eyes and pray for an inspiration. I'm foxed, I admit it."

Somewhere near the Tiber, Kate muttered to herself. The daylight was fading inexorably. Although the speedometer needle touched a hundred kilometres, it seemed to be almost dark when they got back into Rome.

The Pantheon, Kate muttered, the Colosseum, Hadrian's Arch, the Baths of Caracalla, the Catacombs, the Appian Way. . . . Where was her inspiration to come from? Where was the name that held a clue?

Not these ancient monuments. Some modern place, some connection with today or yesterday. Connection! The telephone! The mysterious number Mrs. Dix had asked for, seemingly at random, which had proved to be a cardboard box factory. But was it indeed such a place?

Tense with excitement, Kate sat forward, murmuring numbers to herself.

"What is it?" Lucian asked a little disturbed.

"The telephone number. I can't remember it. I wrote it down, though. Where did I write it? Oh, I know. On the telephone pad at the flat. Oh, Lord, I'll have to ring Mrs. Peebles. What's the time? Have we time to get a call through to London?"

"I don't follow one word of what you're talking about, but if you want to call London, Giovanni can get some priority. I don't think I told you. Giovanni is a member of Interpol. But that's not for general consumption. A telephone, Giovanni. *Pronto!*"

Mrs. Peebles' high-pitched and uncomprehending voice at the other end of the wire was maddeningly aggravating. Kate had to repeat slowly and patiently what she wanted, all the time watching the dying light and praying Mrs. Peebles had not torn the top sheet off the telephone pad.

William could look after himself pretty capably, she kept reminding herself.

Even if the moon rose before Mrs. Peebles' dull brain rose equally to the occasion.

"You mean these numbers written here," came back her incredulous voice. "You're phoning me all the way from Rome for these little bits of numbers! Your writing's horrible. I can hardly read it. I'll have to get my glasses."

"Please, Mrs. Peebles! Hurry!"

There was a short interval, then the voice came back, laboriously reading.

"Good," Kate said. "Good. Thank you, Mrs. Peebles."

"When will you be back?"

"I don't know. I'll let you know."

"Things have been quiet since you left. No scrabblers at the window. Oh, a friend of yours called with a cat. I sent her to—"

Regretfully Kate cut her off.

"Here's the number. Find out what place it belongs to. It's only a hunch. They said it was a box factory."

"It may be near the Tiber," Lucian said. He handed the slip of paper to Giovanni who began to make another telephone call. In a few moments he had the address. It was a factory, he said, and it was in the poorer area. They'd go out and take a look at it. He added doubtfully that the signorina might wait, but the signorina said firmly that she was going, too, and was in the car ahead of both the men.

It was only a hunch, she told herself, but now she was tense with apprehension and hope.

Through a labyrinth of streets and then down a meaner, darker one where the shabby cafés and houses dwindled to a space of waste ground, and beyond that a large building that looked derelict. The moon, flame-coloured and enormous, was just beginning to rise. Kate hypnotically watched it appear over the low, uneven rooftops. Then, as Giovanni slid the car to a noiseless stop, she scrambled out after him, and picked her way over the rubble to the deserted hulk of the building.

"Kate—" Lucian whispered.

"Don't say it. I'm coming." She added sensibly, "The place isn't derelict because it still has a telephone connection and someone who answers the telephone. Let's look for the office part."

The main doors were locked and bolted. Lucian tried them carefully, but there was no hope of getting in that way. The windows were boarded over. Another smaller door failed to give access, but around at the back, where suddenly there was a gleam of water in the distance and the smell of its coldness on the rising wind, there was another window, unboarded.

Giovanni's efforts to open it were unsuccessful. Suddenly he smashed a pane of glass with what Kate realized shakily was a gun. The noise was shatteringly loud, but when it had died away the dark building was utterly silent. Giovanni thrust his hand in, opened a catch, and slid up the window. In a second he was inside and Lucian had followed.

"Wait there, Kate," begged Lucian.

"Here! All alone!" she asked incredulously, and clambered after them into the damp, cold darkness.

Giovanni produced a torch and shone it cautiously. They were inside the main part of the factory which was obviously disused. There were boxes manufactured and unsold, piled high, and some pieces of rusty machinery. The place looked as if it had been out of use for a long time, probably since early in the war when the business had been closed down or failed.

But somewhere there was a telephone.

It was Kate who found the door. She leaned against it accidentally in the darkness, as Giovanni, with his torch, and Lucian following him, picked their way across the rotted and uneven floor.

It gave behind her and she fell inward. . . .

A hand circled her throat, and something hard stuck into her ribs.

"Stay right where you are!" came William's voice, harshly.

As quick as a flash she twisted herself free.

"William, you *clot*!"

"Good God, it's you, Kate!" William said in surprise.

"Yes, it's me and you've nearly choked me. Where are some lights, for heaven's sake!"

Lucian was there, and Giovanni with his torch, but William had reached over and turned on a glaring, unshaded light in the room into which Kate had stumbled.

"Don't mind the bodies," he said laconically.

One, the small, slim, light-footed man with the Chinese-yellow skin, lay face upwards, his eyes closed, his chest rising and falling with the heavy breathing of unconsciousness. The other, neatly trussed, like a parcel, was lying half under the desk. William, with the bruised face and rapidly blackening eyes that Kate had expected, was grinning cheerfully.

"These birds made a mistake about my left-hook. I haven't tried it out since Varsity days. Well, what did they expect, giving me a lift into Rome and bringing me to this dump. I admit I had a bit of a time getting free." He grimaced as he rubbed deeply wealed wrists. "I won't go into that now, but I'd just made it when I heard you people breaking in and I thought I had to take on another half dozen. As an editor, I'm a bit rusty."

"You shouldn't have trusted them!" Kate stormed. "I told Lucian you'd do something idiotic like that. If you knew the search we've had."

"Was I up for ransom or something?" William asked, interestedly.

"Well, don't gloat over it," Kate snapped. She moved back a little. "Are those men dead?"

"The Chink's breathing," said William. "The other one was tougher. He nearly had me, that one."

"Major Dix," Kate whispered fearfully, as Lucian and Giovanni knelt over the silent, trussed figure, dragging him out from beneath the desk and turning his face to the light.

"Oh, no, it's not!" she gasped, turning white. "It's Johnnie Lambert!"

Lucian loosened the gag around Johnnie's mouth.

"I think your first guess is right, Kate. Major Dix."

The pale, protuberant eyes blinked up at Kate. There was no heartiness in them now, only an enormous disgust and contempt.

"The next time you fall in love, Kate," he said, in the clipped, cultured voice that made the familiar hearty tones she remembered a burlesque, "do me a favour and choose someone who isn't an ex-heavyweight champion."

"I'm not in love," Kate began automatically.

William's swollen eyes looked at her.

"Aren't you?" he said belligerently. "Then I promise you soon will be. If we can't get a marriage licence by tomorrow then we do without it. Do you agree, Kate?"

Quite suddenly and helplessly, Kate began to cry. She gasped through her tears, "I'm only crying because I'm happy. It's absolutely the only time I cry. Yes, yes, I long to do without a marriage licence. In the meantime, that is. . . ."

Giovanni was at the telephone, the instrument that so recently had been used for the threats to William's life. The yellow-faced man on the floor stirred and groaned. Major Dix, alias Johnnie Lambert, looked up into Lucian's narrowed, ruthless eyes, and his too-plump and ruddy face seemed to wither. His slack lips worked. He was no longer the casual, good-natured, rather noisy companion of an evening out; nor was he the absent husband for whom Mrs. Dix hungered and was eternally faithful to; nor Rosita's dashing lover, giving her back her family home and the luxuries she demanded. Even less was he the cool, clever brain behind an organization of international jewel thieves. He was a man facing his supreme test of courage and failing dismally.

"Don't call the police," he begged. "I'll pay you. I'll make it up to your sister and her kids. Dalrymple's death was an accident. So was my wife's. She got difficult. She'd been drinking and her heart was bad. I'd have told her about buying the villa for Rosita. Damn Rosita, anyway. Damn all women. Just undo these cords, there's a good fellow. I'll pay you. I'm not a poor man. . . ."

Lucian lifted his head. His profile was austere, unyielding, devoid of emotion.

"The moon's up," he said, in a voice of deadly quiet.

Johnnie began to struggle violently. His eyes flickered from Lucian's avenging face to Kate's. Their fear was replaced by a look of rage. "It was you, you interfering little bitch!" he said thickly.

Then he began to sob.

Kate thrust her fingers in her ears and blindly ran into the dark outer room. William followed her. At the broken window he caught her and helped her out. As she swayed, in the cool moonlight, he took her in his arms and drew her into the shadow of the building.

"Kate!" he whispered. "Kate, Kate, Kate!"

They were still there, in the shadow, when the police car drew up. Presently the footsteps, coming and going, ceased. The car started up and swept away. Lucian called tentatively, "Kate!" There was a laugh that was Giovanni's, then Giovanni's car started and moved away. After that it was quiet. The moon, no longer flame-coloured, but a pure, clear yellow, made the distant patch of water gleam. And it was warm and safe for ever in William's arms.

NINETEEN

THE SUN SHONE again in the morning. The chestnuts clung to the last remnants of their vanity, and with deliberation relinquished another ill-spared handful of leaves. The trams rumbled by, the street vendors shouted in their shrill, long-drawn-out syllables, and the great city hid its memories beneath an unshadowed exterior.

Lucian found Kate and William still at breakfast.

"Well, you two! Not married yet?"

"We decided we couldn't disappoint my stepmother and

Mrs. Peebles by depriving them of a wedding," Kate said serenely. "Besides, William can't take two black eyes into a respectable church, and I don't look so madly beautiful myself. But no one can stop us enjoying Rome. We're going to sit like lizards on old stone walls for hours and hours. And later of course we have to throw coins in the fountain, or that darling receptionist will shed tears of disappointment. Oh, and we've had a telephone call from Miss Squires. She says she can't locate Francesca, but she's met a village constable who is awfully helpful, and oddly enough is even more besotted about cats than she is."

"You're talking too much, Kate," said William. His grin was slightly lopsided because of a swollen cheek. "But all that she says is more or less true. How, by the way, are the casualties?"

"In the right hands," said Lucian briefly. "There are a few accessories to the fact to be rounded up, in Paris and London, but that should be child's play, comparatively. The police have located Rosita, spitting like Miss Squires' cat. The case will be a *cause célèbre*, I fear. I wonder if you two lizards can spare half an hour from your sun-bathing this morning."

"Of course," Kate agreed. She added ingenuously, "I'm going to like you again, Lucian, when you get that avenging look off your facc." But her hand crept into William's and was lost in its capacious grip.

"Better come to our wedding, old chap," said William.

"Thanks, I'd like to. Giovanni's outside. Can you be ready in ten minutes or so? This won't take long. I thought you'd like to be there. Kate, anyway."

"Where?" Kate asked curiously.

But Lucian had turned away, and even later in the car he made no explanation.

Giovanni drove in his usual swift, hair-raising way to the outskirts of the city. Then he took a turn Kate knew. She recognized the beginning of the Appian Way, and the street into which they came was disturbingly familiar. Outside Gianetta's house he stopped.

"We're a little early," said Lucian. Then, "No, we're not. They're coming now."

Another car had turned into the street and was drawing up behind them. As the inevitable heads began to peer out of windows, Kate gave a cry. She reached for the door and throwing it open leapt out of the car.

"Francesca! Francesca!"

The little girl in the stiffly starched white dress who got composedly out of the other car didn't answer or smile. She came towards Kate, her large, dark eyes full of accusation.

"Where is Pepita?" she asked in careful English.

"Oh! She's at the hotel! I didn't know I was going to see you this morning. No one told me." Kate could not restrain herself then. She threw her arms around the child. She was laughing and crying. "Francesca, it's just so wonderful to see you again. Everyone tried to tell me you weren't real. But look at you! Fatter than ever. What have you been eating in England? Ravioli?"

"So that's the dream child," said William. "Blue bow and all. Incredible!"

"Pepita!" said Francesca stolidly.

The young man who got out of the car after her said in a pleasant Cockney voice, "She would wear those clothes. Didn't half make a fuss. Mrs. Dalrymple gave up in the end. If we hadn't been flying I don't think we'd have persuaded her to come at all. What is it she has to do?"

Lucian spoke swiftly to Francesca in her own language. She listened, blinking her great eyes. Then with decision she shook her head. She spoke in a high, definite voice. Lucian tried to reason with her. Giovanni joined in persuasively. Francesca shook her head stubbornly.

"Pepita!" she said.

Giovanni shrugged. Lucian sighed.

"I'm sorry, Kate. We'll have to dash back to the hotel for that wretched doll. She won't do what we want until she gets it. The rest of you can wait here. Sorry, Sergeant. But you know by now what you're dealing with."

The young police sergeant nodded. "If I'd been you, Miss,

darned if I wouldn't have pushed her off the train myself. It's just as well aeroplane windows don't open."

Francesca, gazing from one to another, gave her faint Mona Lisa smile and folded her plump hands on her plump stomach.

When Lucian and Kate returned to the scene some thirty minutes later, however, they found that Pepita as a bribe was no longer necessary. Francesca glanced at her indifferently and turned away. She was sitting on the side of the gutter talking animatedly to William, her plump face breaking into a series of delighted dimpled smiles.

Never, thought Kate furiously, never once had Francesca smiled like that for her.

"What are you telling her?" she demanded.

William gave his slow, maddening grin.

"That when she's grown up and wears these fascinating bits of glass around her neck I'll marry her."

He opened his large hand and there, winking and glittering fabulously in the sunlight, were the diamonds, undoubtedly the stolen and broken-up necklace of the Venetian Contessa.

"Where—" began Lucian.

Giovanni burst into a roar of laughter.

Francesca chattered animatedly, spreading her skirts and preening herself like a little peacock.

"Just here," William said, poking his fingers into the outlet drain of the long-dry gutter. "Poor kids in Rome always play in the gutter. And Francesca thought rightly that these were just a handful of stones. Why should Pepita be cluttered up with them?" Then he looked rueful. "But now I seem to have sown the seeds of vanity. I've told her they make her look pretty."

"Even with two black eyes you have quite a way with girls, haven't you," Kate said scathingly. "Just for that you can help me look after Francesca until her mother gets back."

"Kate! This is our honeymoon!"

"Or we can take her with us on the train back to England."

"Heaven forbid!" William exclaimed.

Francesca gave her unexpected and enchanting dimpled smile.

"No spik *Inglese,*" she said, and waited for the usual looks of frustration that would follow her flat and inexorable statement.

When, this time, they didn't come she looked a little puzzled, then philosophically shrugged her plump shoulders, dismissing the adult world which had never particularly interested her, and turned at last to be reunited with Pepita.

Cat's Prey

'From the first page of all her books, Dorothy Eden never fails to intrigue – *Books and Bookmen*

Cat's Prey

When Antonia arrived in Auckland, the voice that warned her of danger over the telephone sounded heavy and menacing. It decoyed her away from the hotel—and while she was away someone searched her room.

When she eventually reached her cousin Simon's house, were the noises she heard in the night those of an imprisoned and terrified woman, or just echoes in a mind stretched to exhaustion? Surely she wasn't imagining the light in the deserted wing . . .

Melbury Square

'This colourful, romantic period novel is one of the best yet'—*Publishers Weekly*

Melbury Square

Debutante Maud Lucie was somewhat different from her contemporaries in Edwardian London. Though thoroughly spoiled and a little self-centred, she inherited from her artist father a zest for life and a rather flamboyant way of living it.

Ironically, it was her father's last-minute intervention which prevented her marrying a romantic young poet and this was to prove a cruel stroke of fate. Eventually pressured into a disastrous marriage and finding a total lack of *rapport* with her growing daughter, Maud watches the passing of the years and the changing life-styles, which completely alter the character of her beloved Melbury Square.

And then, alone and unwanted in her twilight years, she encounters a pair of brazen young people whose outrageous behaviour provokes a final, characteristic act of flamboyance.

The Sleeping Bride

It was unthinkable that Lydia should admit, even to herself, that she had fallen in love with her sister's fiancé . . .

Aurora was the kind of girl every man admires—beautiful, glamorous and exciting. And her fiancé, Philip, was everything a girl could want in a man.

When Aurora disappeared on the eve of the wedding, Lydia found herself thrown into turmoil and mystery, and forced to answer some questions that seemed incapable of solution.

Could she throw convention to the winds and love a man already betrothed to another?

Where had Aurora gone—and why?

Most important of all, who was the vicious villain who was trying to poison their lives?

It was only after great effort that the answers to these questions came, and gave Lydia a new sense of purpose and a new hope for life.